To Annie

with love

[signature]

1985

HUNGRY FOR LOVE

Araminta Sinclair is horrified when she
learns her brother Sir Harry Sinclair
has lost £600 gaming, to the Marquis
of Wayne.
She offers to give up the small sum
collected for her début in London and
then has an inspiration as to how
they can obtain the rest.
Her father, the previous Baronet,
a gourmet and an epicure
insisted on his daughter becoming an
exceptionally fine cook.
How Araminta enlists the help of
General Sir Alexander Bracknell, one
of Wellington's Commanders, how
there is a bet that her cooking can
rival that of Carême – the Prince
Regent's Master Chef – and how her
deception brings her heart-break and
finally happiness is told in this
dramatic novel by Barbara
Cartland.

Barbara Cartland

Hungry for Love

ROBERT HALE · LONDON

Copyright © Barbara Cartland 1976

This edition 1985

ISBN 0 7090 2328 6

Robert Hale Limited
Clerkenwell House
Clerkenwell Green
London EC1R 0HT

Printed in Great Britain by
Photobooks (Bristol) Ltd.
and bound by
W.B.C. Bookbinders Ltd.

ABOUT THE AUTHOR

Barbara Cartland, the world's most famous romantic novelist, who is also an historian, playwright, lecturer, political speaker and television personality, has now written over 370 books and sold over 370 million over the world.

She has also had many historical works published and has written four autobiographies as well as the biographies of her mother and that of her brother, Ronald Cartland, who was the first Member of Parliament to be killed in the last war. This work has a preface by Sir Winston Churchill and has just been republished with an introduction by Sir Arthur Bryant.

'Love at the Helm', a recent novel, was written with the help and inspiration of the late Admiral of the Fleet, the Earl Mountbatten of Burma. This is being sold for the Mountbatten Memorial Trust.

Miss Cartland in 1978 sang an Album of Love Songs with the Royal Philharmonic Orchestra.

In 1976 by writing twenty-one books, she broke the world record and has continued for the following seven years with 24, 20, 23, 24 25 and 23. In the Guinness Book of Records she is listed as the world's top-selling author.

In private life Barbara Cartland, who is a Dame of the Order of St. John of Jerusalem, Chairman of the St. John Council in Hertfordshire and Deputy President of the St. John Ambulance Brigade, has fought for better conditions and salaries for Midwives and Nurses.

She has championed the cause for old people, had the law altered regarding gypsies and founded the first Romany Gypsy camp in the world.

Barbara Cartland is deeply interested in Vitamin Therapy, and is President of the National Association for Health.

Her designs "Decorating with Love" are being sold all over

the U.S.A. and the National Home Fashions League made her, in 1981, "Woman of Achievement".

Barbara Cartland's Romances (Book of Cartoons) has been published in seventy-five newspapers in the United States and throughout the world.

CHAPTER ONE

1871

"Harry, how could you do anything so crazy?"

"I know, Araminta, I have no excuse except that I was somewhat foxed!"

"But at this moment .. when we have not a penny to spare!"

"I know, I know," Sir Harry Sinclair agreed despairingly.

He was an extremely handsome, well-built young man of twenty-one.

Dressed in the height of fashion, with the tight yellow pantaloons which were the mode amongst the Bucks and Dandies of St. James's, with his cut-away coat which fitted without a wrinkle, the points of his collar high above his square chin, he was a figure to make any woman's heart beat faster.

But the look on the face of his sister Araminta was one of dismay as she asked in a voice that was deliberately expressionless:

"How .. much did you .. lose?"

"£600!"

Araminta gave a little shriek. Then, as if she fought for self-control, she walked to the window to stare out into the quiet Bloomsbury street.

"I must have been mad, I see that now," her brother said behind her, "but Wayne had been winning all the evening. He had had the luck of the Devil, and by the law of averages he should have lost that particular hand."

There was no response from Araminta and after a moment he went on:

"He always sits there looking so cursed superior, as if even

9

to win was beneath his condescension. There is something about him which gets under my skin."

"Who are you talking about?" Araminta asked in a dull voice.

"The Marquis of Wayne. I do not suppose you have heard of him, but he is a leader of fashion. The Dandies copy his cravats and the Bucks try to emulate his feats as a Corinthian."

"You sound as if you dislike him."

"I hate him!" Harry replied passionately. "As I told you, Araminta, he gets under my skin. He walks into White's as if he had bought the place, and God knows there are a number of Members who are more important than he is."

"I cannot imagine why that should upset you to the point of challenging him at cards!"

"I know now it was a wild, insane thing to do," Harry admitted. "Wayne always wins! They laugh about it in the Club. But there was something in the way he looked at me, when I sat down at the table."

"Explain what you .. mean."

"Oh, I suppose I was just being nonsensical, but he made me feel as if I was a country-bumpkin – a green-horn – which undoubtedly I am!"

Harry Sinclair gave a little gulp.

"I wanted to assert myself, and look at the mess it has landed me in!"

"Not only you," Araminta said quietly.

Her brother threw himself down in a chair and put his hands up to his face.

"Help me, Araminta. You have every right to be cross, but for Heaven's sake, help me!"

The appeal in his voice melted Araminta's heart. She never could resist her handsome brother anyway.

She ran across the room to kneel down beside his chair.

"It is all right, Harry," she said soothingly as if he was a child. "We will see this through together. You know you have the family behind you."

"Mama .." Harry said, taking his hand from his face.

"Yes, I know," Araminta replied, "but we will not tell her .. at any rate not until we have to."

She paused before she asked:

"How long have we in which to .. find the .. money?"

Harry's voice sounded almost strangled in his throat as he replied:

"Two weeks."

"Oh, no!" Araminta cried. "It is impossible! How can we find such a large sum in that time?"

She sat back on her heels as she spoke and looked up at her brother and he looked back at her.

Their eyes met and they were both calculating! They were both acutely aware of their financial position.

When their father, Sir Gilbert Sinclair died from the wounds he had received at Waterloo, they had found that his estate amounted to little more than debts.

Their grandfather, the second Baronet, had been a wild gambler who had dispersed the family fortunes and left his eldest son little but a dilapidated Manor House and a few acres of land near Ampthill in Bedfordshire.

Fortunately, Lady Sinclair had an allowance from her father.

He had disapproved of the marriage and refused to settle any money on his daughter.

"To prevent your husband being able to play ducks and drakes with my money," he had said, "what you receive from me will be paid quarterly, and I will not give you one penny more, not if you are starving in the gutter!"

It was Lady Sinclair's very small fortune which had enabled them to live frugally, but in comparative comfort, in Bedfordshire.

It was a poor County and there were not a great number of expenses, not even for a man of rank.

However, Sir Gilbert and his wife were so happy together that they were quite content with the unpretentious social life they could enjoy with their neighbours and did not miss the extravagance and luxury of London.

But Harry was different.

Harry was young and he found Bedfordshire excessively

dull – which indeed it was – and the horses that his father rode too slow for his liking.

He had come to London at the beginning of the year and set himself up in lodgings which he had described to his family as being 'well up to scratch'.

He had also, through the sponsorship of the Duke of Bedford, been elected a member of White's Club. This, Araminta now could not help thinking, was really his downfall.

White's was the most exclusive and the smartest Club in London.

It was not only the haunt of all the dashing young Bucks and blades, but also of politicians, statesmen and the Regent himself.

As Harry reported gleefully in his letters home, the Duke of Wellington had only been elected in 1812 – '*so I am not*,' he added, '*such a very young member, except of course in years*'.

Situated in St. James's Street, White's counted amongst its members the brilliant wits of the *Beau Monde* such as Lord Alvanley and, until he was obliged to leave England the previous year owing to his debts, the inimitable Beau Brummell.

Charles James Fox, whose speeches in the House of Commons packed the Chamber quicker than any other orator's was a member, so was Sir Robert Peel who was introducing a Police Force to London, and the 6th Earl of Shaftesbury, who harrowed Society with reports of the cruelty inflicted on climbing boys and the iniquities of Flash Houses.

In fact, in White's one could find every type of character and personality that made London Society the most glittering and the most envied of all Europe.

But it was also in White's that the most compulsive gambling took place, and where great fortunes were lost and gained night after night.

Harry had been overwhelmingly grateful to the Duke of Bedford for introducing him to this gentleman's Paradise. But Araminta could not help thinking that perhaps it would have been wiser if her brother had been forced to wait until he had found his feet in London.

"£600!" she said aloud. "Have you anything left of your allowance?"

They had decided on their father's death to divide the income which their mother received every quarter.

Harry took one half and the other half was, with a great deal of scrimping and saving, enough for Lady Sinclair and her two daughters to live on.

There had, however, this year been the problem of Araminta's début.

It should in fact have taken place the previous year when she was just eighteen, but as they were in deep mourning it was impossible for them to consider entertainment of any sort.

Araminta was now nearing nineteen. She had resigned herself to appearing only at the local Hunt Ball and a few other festivities in Bedfordshire.

Then suddenly the Duchess of Bedford, who was friendly with Lady Sinclair, had told her that the Duke was prepared to offer them a furnished house for the Season so that Araminta could make her début in London.

This astounding news had taken them all by surprise, but there was no question of refusing such a generous offer.

"The Duchess has even said, dearest, that she will introduce you to Almack's," Lady Sinclair said ecstatically, "and under the auspices of Her Grace's patronage, we may be sure that all the fashionable hostesses will invite you to their Balls."

For the first time in their lives Araminta and her younger sister Caro were leaving the quietness of Bedfordshire.

Woburn Abbey was only a short distance from their home, but they had in fact seen very little of the Duke and Duchess of Bedford who lived mostly in London.

"It is one thing to be given a house, Mama," Araminta said, "but you know as well as I do that I cannot appear in London wearing the gowns I have made myself. I should be laughed at and undoubtedly labelled a 'milk-maid', or something equally rude."

"You may be surprised to hear it, but I have already thought of that!" Lady Sinclair said in her gentle voice. "Actually, although we have never told you so, your father and I

13

have been saving for many years for your début and later your marriage."

"Saving, Mama?" Araminta exclaimed in surprise.

"It was very difficult because, as you know, we had so little," Lady Sinclair said with a smile. "Sometimes we sold fruit from the garden, and once your father had a good day at the races and we put aside half his winnings."

Her eyes misted for a moment when she spoke of her husband but she went on bravely.

"There were other opportunities too, and we have collected enough not only for your gowns, Araminta, but also to do a small amount of entertaining in the house we have been loaned."

"I can hardly believe it, Mama," Araminta cried in astonishment.

"I am not as feather-witted as you and Harry seem to think!" Lady Sinclear replied with a touch of pride.

It was true that while they loved their mother, the children found her at times somewhat scatter-brained.

She found it difficult to remember engagements or to recall the names of neighbours and acquaintances unless she knew them very well.

She was invariably late for meals because either she was immersed in painting one of the water-colours which had always delighted her husband, or she had started to pick flowers to make a pot-pourri just when she should have returned to the house.

She was in many ways like a child who runs after every brilliant butterfly.

But because her happiness was centred in her home, her children tried to protect her from anything that was ugly and disagreeable, and always from financial difficulties.

It was therefore amazing to Araminta that her mother should have not only thought ahead, but *had* also made a sustained effort over the years to save towards her début.

She was even more astonished when she found that the sum had reached the incredible figure of £110!

"Do you think it will be enough, dearest?" Lady Sinclair asked a little anxiously.

"Of course, Mama! But I must not spend anything like the whole of it on myself. There is Caro to think of! She is already seventeen and perhaps next year the Duchess will remember that it will be her turn to go to London."

"You're very sweet and unselfish, dearest," Lady Sinclair answered fondly, "but I am hoping, Araminta, that perhaps while you are in London you will find a husband."

For a moment Araminta looked startled, then she said quietly:

"Yes, of course, Mama. Then I should be able to help Caro. She will be very beautiful and she must have her chance."

"You are both outstandingly lovely," Lady Sinclair said. "And your Papa and I always regretted that our home should be in Bedfordshire, because it is undoubtedly an extremely dull County."

But due to the kindness of the Duke, they found themselves installed in an attractive house in Russell Square which he used to lend to his relatives when they desired to visit London.

'I have exactly two months,' Araminta thought when they arrived on the 8th April.

Two months in which not only to enjoy herself but also to remember that every débutante hoped to receive an offer of marriage if possible from a wealthy suitor!

But now Araminta realised only the second day after her arrival that her plans were collapsing like a pack of cards.

She had known as soon as Harry came down to breakfast that something was amiss.

He looked tired but that would be due, she thought, to the late nights he enjoyed in London and the amount of wine he had consumed.

It was to be expected that he should wish to live the same life as other young men of his age.

But she had glanced at him a little apprehensively as, instead of taking the cup of coffee she offered him, he walked to the sideboard and poured himself some brandy.

She had said nothing because, after all, Harry was now the head of the family and his own master, and if he wished to drink brandy in the morning it was not for her to criticise him.

At the same time, perceptively, she sensed that something was very wrong and she wondered apprehensively what it could be.

Harry had arranged to stay with them last night and the night they arrived, so as to help them settle into the house. Also because he knew it would give his mother so much pleasure.

Today he was due to return to his lodgings where Araminta was well aware he enjoyed not only his independence but also the attention of an excellent valet he had employed to look after him.

It was as soon as Lady Sinclair left the breakfast-room that Harry had told Araminta of the trouble he was in.

"£600!" she said again beneath her breath.

"I have been thinking," Harry said, "that if I give up my lodgings and dismiss my servant, that would save some money."

"I asked you how much you had left of your allowance."

There was a pause before Harry said defensively:

"I have nothing left of this quarter's."

"Oh, Harry!"

Araminta bit back the words which rose to her lips.

There was no use in being cross, she thought. If it was spent, it was spent; no amount of recrimination would bring it back.

"I shall get something for my horses."

"Your horses?" Araminta asked.

"That is why I am hard-up," he answered. "I had the chance of buying two really fine animals. They belonged to an acquaintance who was going abroad. He let me have them cheap."

He paused before he added:

"I shall get more than I paid for them."

"How much can you raise all . . together?"

"I have lain awake all night doing sums in my head," Harry replied, "and I imagine that with the horses, Papa's watch, cuff-links and tie-pin which Mama gave me before I came to London, I could raise about £250."

"You must not tell Mama," Araminta said quickly. "Not about the tie-pin, nor Papa's watch."

"No, of course not!"

"That is nearly half," Araminta said, "and there is £110 which Mama has saved for my gowns. I think I told you about it."

"But, Araminta, I cannot take your money!" Harry protested.

Araminta gave a little laugh that was almost a sob.

"You can hardly expect me to dance gaily at Almack's while you are languishing in a Debtors' prison!"

"It will not come to that," Harry said. "At least I do not think so."

There was some doubt in his tone.

"You mean that the Marquis will not sue you if you cannot meet your debt to him?"

"It would be an unprecedented thing for one gentleman to do to another," Harry answered. "At the same time, you know as well as I do, Araminta, that a gambling debt is one of honour. To default means I should be forced to resign from White's with ignominy, and it is doubtful if any of its members would ever speak to me again."

"That must never happen," Araminta said firmly.

"I do not see how I can prevent it," Harry admitted despondently.

He put his hands up to his face again.

"Oh, God Araminta, how could I have been such a damned fool? How could I have made such an absolute hash of everything?"

"I suppose if you .. pleaded with the Marquis .. if you told him the circumstances .. ?"

"Plead with the Marquis of Wayne?" Harry asked derisively. "I might just as well plead with the Rock of Gibraltar! He is as hard as granite, with not an ounce of kindness in his whole make-up. He may be admired for his appearance, his possessions and his achievements, but I do not suppose there is one person in the whole of London who really likes him."

"But why?" Araminta enquired.

"God knows," Harry replied. "There is just something about him. His air of superiority. I am not the only one who finds him insufferable."

He paused before he added reflectively:

"He behaves as if we were all beneath contempt."

"Then if we cannot appeal to him," Araminta said, "we shall have to raise every penny we can, and promise him the rest in instalments."

"He will not like that," Harry muttered.

"It does not matter what he likes," Araminta said. "It is a question of what we are able to give him. Now, if we have £250 from you, the £110 which Mama has put aside for my gowns, and I suppose there must be £30 or £40 in the Bank, then we have nearly £400."

"We have to live until next quarterday."

"Yes, I know," Araminta agreed miserably.

She stiffened suddenly.

"There is Mama's engagement ring!"

"Oh, no, I cannot ask her for that," Harry demurred.

"It must be worth nearly £100," Araminta said. "She has always kept it, however hard-up she and Papa were, because she loved it so much."

"It is the last thing I would ask Mama to give me."

"I am sure she would part with it willingly rather than allow you to be disgraced publicly."

Araminta rose to her feet to walk restlessly across the room.

"If only we had something else we could sell, something we could do."

"I have been thinking that myself," Harry replied. "It is ridiculous, Araminta, that an education like mine fits a man for nothing except a capacity for spending money. I suppose I might find employment grooming horses or driving a Mail-Coach."

"I am sure that would not bring in very much."

"Then what can we do?" Harry asked desperately.

18

Quite suddenly Araminta stood still in the centre of the room.

She looked very beautiful in the sunshine coming through the long, square-paned windows.

It lit the gold of her hair and glinted in her worried grey eyes before she exclaimed in a voice which seemed to echo round the walls:

"I have an idea! Oh, Harry, I have a really wonderful idea!"

. . . . . .

General Sir Alexander Bracknell was reading *The Morning Post* in his lodgings in Half Moon Street when his valet came into the room.

"There's a lady to see you, Sir," he said in the crisp military tones of a man who has once served in the Army.

The General looked up in surprise.

"A lady?" he questioned.

"A young lady, Sir. Says it's of the utmost importance she should speak with you."

"In which case I must undoubtedly see her," the General replied. "Show her in, Hawkins."

"Very good, Sir."

Hawkins marched smartly from the room, and the General put down *The Morning Post* and pulled the lapels of his coat into place.

He had been noted as being one of the smartest commanders in Wellington's army, but he was remembered not so much for his brains, as for his popularity.

There had been two of Wellington's Generals who had been not only admired but also loved by the troops.

One had been Lord Hill, who was always known as 'Daddy Hill' to those who had served with him in the Peninsula, and the other was General Bracknell, who was called by all and sundry 'Uncle Alex'.

He thought now as he waited that the woman who had called to see him was probably the wife, the widow or the mother of one of the soldiers under his command.

Although the war had been over for nearly two years, hardly a week passed in which there was not someone pleading for his assistance or, in far too many cases, begging for financial support.

Only those who were close to the General were aware that he could afford very little in the way of luxuries owing to the fact that his wife had for the last five years been insane.

The General's pension and everything he had accumulated during his distinguished career in the Army was spent in providing accommodation for Lady Bracknell and paying doctors who failed hopelessly to better her condition.

It was therefore a little apprehensively that the General awaited his caller, thinking it was unfortunate that she should have arrived so early, since otherwise he would already have left the house for his invariable constitutional walk in Hyde Park.

The door opened.

"Miss Araminta Sinclair, Sir!"

Araminta stood smiling in the doorway before she hurried across the room towards the General, both hands outstretched.

She looked exceedingly pretty in a high-crowned bonnet which tied under her chin, but the General was too well-versed in the social world not to realise that although she looked charming, both her gown and her bonnet were very countrified.

"Araminta, my dear!" he exclaimed as he rose to his feet. "This is indeed a pleasure!"

"I was so afraid that you might not be at home," Araminta said. "Oh, Uncle Alex, I had to see you!"

"Harry told me that you were arriving in London, and I intended to give myself the pleasure of calling on your mother this afternoon."

"She will be delighted to see you," Araminta said, "but it was important for me to speak to you alone."

The General drew her towards an old but comfortable sofa which stood by the fire-place.

"What is the trouble?" he asked.

Araminta hesitated a moment, then she said:

"We have always believed, Uncle Alex, that you know everyone in the fashionable world."

The General looked a little puzzled, but he said gently:

"People are very kind to me, Araminta, and I suppose I can say without boasting that I am invited to almost all the fashionable houses and to most of the Receptions and Assemblies."

He gave a rather ruthful laugh as he added:

"At my age, retired and with no family, there is little else for me to do except go to my Club."

"Which is White's!" Araminta said in a hard little voice.

"Yes, White's," the General replied, "and I am very glad that Harry was accepted as a member. The Duke of Bedford proposed him and I seconded him. There was no question after that of his not being elected."

"And Harry was so thrilled and pleased to be a member," Araminta said. "At the same time, Uncle Alex, it is because of White's that he is in such trouble."

The General stiffened.

"Gambling?" he asked.

"I am afraid so."

There was an expression on the General's face which Araminta did not understand for a moment. Then she gave a little cry.

"Oh, no, Uncle Alex! No, I was not thinking of that! You know that we would never ask you for money whatever happened! I need your help in a very different way."

She knew that almost imperceptibly the General relaxed as he said:

"If there is anything I can do to help, Araminta, you know I am yours to command."

"I knew you would not fail me, Uncle Alex," Araminta said. "You were so wonderful when Papa died, and I think he worshipped you. He always said that the troops would have followed you into hell and I am sure that was true."

"You are embarrassing me, my dear," the General replied, "but I was very fond of your father and, as you well know, I love you and Caro. But tell me about Harry."

"He has lost a large sum of money," Araminta said, "and we have a very short time in which to raise it. But, Uncle Alex, I have an idea!"

The General did not reply but his eyes were on Araminta's as she went on:

"You have often stayed with us in Bedfordshire. What would you say was the one thing you most remember about our hospitality?"

The General smiled.

"That is not a very difficult question to answer, Araminta. Your father always provided his guests with superlative food. The really fantastic meals I have had when I have been in your house are unforgettable."

"That is what I hoped you would say," Araminta said, "and do you know who did the cooking after poor old Bouvais died?"

"I half suspected that it was you, Araminta."

"It was!" she nodded. "Papa made Bouvais teach me everything he knew. He always said that he would never be able to afford another French Chef, but he was not going to eat the 'pig-swill' which was served in most English houses."

"Your father was a great epicure!" the General said. "I always thought it was a pity he could not afford to entertain on a larger scale."

"Perhaps it was a good thing," Araminta smiled. "We should all have grown extremely fat. But you did enjoy our food whenever you came to stay?"

"I thought it was more than delectable," the General replied. "Your father was a very lucky man to have such a talented daughter."

"It is my one talent," Araminta said, "and I think at the moment the one thing that is saleable."

The General looked at her in surprise as she went on:

"Papa used to tell me how only the very rich could afford French Chefs."

"That is true," the General agreed, "but during first the Revolution, then the Napoleonic wars there was an exodus of private chefs from France when that wretched country had no longer many *grands seigneurs* to employ them."

"And Papa also said," Araminta went on, "that there was great competition in London for French Chefs."

"That is true," the General agreed. "Of course a number of those who came over here did not wish to go into private service and opened Restaurants or are working in the Clubs. The 'Reform' for instance, has a famous kitchen."

"But there is still a demand for really first class cuisine?" Araminta persisted.

"There is always a demand for it," the General answered. "The greatest chef of them all, Antoine Carême, is now employed by the Prince Regent. The food he serves is fantastic, but no better than yours, my dear."

Araminta clasped her hands together.

"Uncle Alex, you are saying exactly what I want to hear! Now you understand why I have come to you."

"I may be very slow-witted," the General said, "but I honestly have not the slightest idea!"

"I want you to recommend me," Araminta said, "to some of your distinguished friends .. as a cook!"

"You must be crazy!" the General ejaculated.

"No, I am being very sensible!" Araminta said. "If we pool all the money we can raise and even, if necessary, ask Mama to sell her engagement ring, we shall still need at least another £100 before we can pay Harry's debt! I am convinced that I can earn that by cooking."

"It is a clever idea," the General conceded, "but are you really suggesting that you should work like a servant in the kitchen of some nobleman's house?"

"Not on a permanent basis," Araminta answered, "but temporarily, perhaps only for one dinner-party in each place. Papa has often told me how expensive a really good meal can be in a high-class Restaurant. I was thinking that I might charge .. £5 for a dinner."

She looked at the General tentatively, thinking he might be horrified at such a suggestion.

"It is certainly an idea," he said slowly, after a moment. "And you cook as well, if not better, than any of the chefs whose employers boast about their achievements."

"Then help me .. please help me, Uncle Alex?" Araminta begged. "Could you say to your friends at White's that you know of a really first-class Chef who would provide them in

23

their own home with a dinner to equal anything they have enjoyed on the Continent?"

Her eyes pleaded with the General as she went on:

"It might be possible in a very short time for me to make enough money to complete the sum that Harry owes."

The General was thinking.

Those who had served under him would have recognised in the knitting of his heavy brows and the way he thrust forward his lower lip, that he was concentrating his extremely astute brain on the problem.

He was remembering that someone, he could not now remember who it was, had said in White's only last week that it was the French cuisine which was saving its country from financial despair.

"What do you mean by that?" an elderly Peer had growled.

"By the Treaty made in November, 1815," was the answer, "France is bound to pay an indemnity of seven hundred million francs within three years."

"We all know that!" the Peer snapped.

"Thanks to the gourmandise of the British who are flocking into France to indulge their stomachs, French cuisine has become a national asset."

The General had not been attending particularly to the argument, but now he thought that in the last few years appreciation of food had been stimulated in England.

There was no doubt that amongst the aristocrats by whom he was constantly entertained, the French technique of cooking had revolutionised the heavy English fare.

The traditional great joints of beef had been beaten into *quenelles,* cut into tournedos, made into filling for vol-au-vents, disguised with succulent sauces.

Puddings were puffed into frothy *soufflés,* sugar was manipulated into *sotelties* in fairy-like shapes of flowers, castles and animals.

Meat, game and fish had each been linked with appropriate sauces, concocted by inspired craftsmen who believed cooking was an art and not just a necessity of life.

And those craftsmen – the Chefs trained in France – were undoubtedly hard to come by.

"You will help me, Uncle Alex?" Araminta asked, interrupting the General's train of thought.

He did not answer and she went on:

"You know there is no-one else I can ask. Papa confided in you, so you are aware that the money Mama receives from her family trustees is paid quarterly, so that there is no chance of any of us touching the capital."

"Yes, I know that," the General agreed.

"Then the only possible solution is for me to earn money as quickly as possible by cooking," Araminta said simply.

"I can see a great many difficulties about it," the General replied weakly.

She knew as he spoke that he would help her.

"Oh, Uncle Alex, I love you!" she cried impulsively, and bent forward to kiss his cheek.

· · · · · ·

White's was filled with gentlemen all holding glasses in their hands and talking over the affairs of the day.

The General, entering the famous morning-room, thought he knew every one present.

The morning-room had been altered six years earlier to provide a second window which had become famous as the bow-window of White's.

It had actually been Beau Brummell who had converted it into a 'Holy of Holies', and it became the centre of fashion for a chosen number.

An ordinary member of the Club would as soon have thought of taking his seat on the Bishop's throne in a Cathedral as appropriating one of the chairs in the sacred window.

Those who sat there looking onto St. James's Street quizzed the passers-by and commented upon them very freely. It was said that White's was the clearing-house for half the current scandals of fashionable London.

Neither of the Regent's brothers ever succeeded in imposing himself on the ultra-exclusive world of fashion – the Duke of Cumberland because he was a blackguard and the Duke of York because he was a bore.

25

But Beau Brummell was always to be found in the bow-window with his particular friends, the Dukes of Argyle, Dorset and Rutland, the Lords Sefton, Alvanley and Plymouth.

The General whenever he entered the morning-room expected to see the Beau himself seated in his familiar seat ruining someone's reputation with a witty sarcasm.

It seemed impossible to think of him lonely and poverty-stricken, eking out an existence in Calais!

But his friends were still in their usual places and the General, looking round him, planning his campaign, chose his ground for attack with the care that had made him a notable commander.

Everyone who caught his eye hailed him.

"Hello, Uncle Alex!" the older members cried good-humouredly.

The General was as popular among them as he was among the young Bucks who said more respectfully:

"Good-evening, General!"

They called him 'Uncle Alex' behind his back and he was flattered that they should do so.

A nickname meant a great deal in this harum-scarum, snob-conscious social world, where a man was accepted because he was liked and not only because his blood was blue and his family-tree a long one.

"Where were you last night?" the General heard Lord Sefton ask Lord Alvanley.

Alvanley was noted as a gourmet besides being a wit.

The members of White's had once offered the prize of a free dinner to whoever could produce the most expensive culinary dish.

Lord Alvanley had won with an entree made of the hearts of three hundred game birds.

There had been thirteen kinds; a hundred snipe, twenty pheasants and so on.

The dish had cost one hundred and eight pounds, five shillings!

"I was at Carlton House," Lord Alvanley answered to Lord Sefton's enquiry.

"Lucky fellow!" his friend remarked. "I was dining at the Palace – a deadly evening! And the food was what you would expect in a second-rate Posting Inn!"

"The King, before he went mad, used to appreciate good food," Lord Alvanley remarked laconically, "but Carême was in his best form! Since he arrived in England, I swear the Regent has put on another two stone!"

This was the opening the General was waiting for and he manoeuvred himself into position.

"I think Carême is good," he said in his deep voice which carried over many battle-fields. "But I know of a Chef who is better."

"Better than Carême?" Lord Alvanley exclaimed.

He spoke loudly and quite a number of those drinking around them stopped to listen.

"Indeed yes," the General said. "But the Chef I am thinking of is too expensive for you young blades. If I could afford him myself, I would confidently challenge anyone to provide a better meal this side of the Channel!'

"Better than Carême?" Lord Alvanley repeated, as if he thought he could not have heard the General aright. "The Regent would have a stroke if he heard you decrying his precious Chef!"

"I dare say," the General replied, "but facts are facts, and I assure you that, while I admit that Carême can supply a meal that is superlative, I have found his master."

"I do not believe it," Lord Sefton said. "Where is this phenomenon? Let us try out his food and judge for ourselves."

"I wish I could afford to invite you to dinner to prove my point," the General said. "But as I have said, my 'phenomenon' is an expensive one!"

"Then I will tell you that we will do," Lord Alvanley said excitedly. "One of us will give a dinner employing your protégé, and we will take a vote at the end of the evening as to whether you are right or wrong, Uncle Alex."

"I shall certainly bet on it," Lord Sefton said.

"So shall I!" Lord Plymouth, who had been listening, interposed.

"The question is, who is to give the dinner?" Lord Alvanley asked tentatively.

The General knew that Lord Alvanley himself would be unable to do so, since being a compulsive gambler, he was deeply in debt.

He had spent over £50,000 since coming into his inheritance, most of it having disappeared like fairy-gold on the green baize tables upstairs.

"I will give the dinner!" a voice said behind the General.

He turned and was unable to prevent himself from starting.

It was the Marquis of Wayne who had spoken, whom he had not even realised was in the room!

Araminta had finally admitted to the General to whom Harry was in debt, and the General had thought that it could not have been more unfortunate.

Wayne was a strange, unpredictable personality. He had many fine attributes and, as the General knew well, he was an excellent soldier.

But he was proud, reserved and in a way insolently repressive to those around him. He had, as Harry had found, an air of superiority which many men found intolerable.

He had never been known to do a kindly action, although he had certainly never been known to commit a dishonourable one.

He was in fact a hard man, and the General, who was exceedingly warm-hearted himself, had found it impossible to like the Marquis, even though he knew it was unfair to judge a man by his rating in popularity.

The list of hosts he had envisaged giving the dinner at which Araminta could show her skill had certainly not included the Marquis of Wayne!

For one thing, the Marquis was known to have a chef who was renowned in the *Beau Monde* as being outstanding.

For another, he was seldom involved in the endless wagers which were notable at White's and which had made the betting-book a uniquely valuable asset of the Club.

But if the General was surprised at the Marquis's intervention, no less were Lord Alvanley and Lord Sefton.

"*You,* Wayne – *you* will give the dinner?" Lord Alvanley exclaimed. "But why? What has happened to Gustave?"

"I dismissed him this morning," the Marquis replied coldly.

"You dismissed him?" Lord Alvanley echoed blankly. "What on earth for?"

"He was stealing," the Marquis answered, "And I object on principle to having thieves in my house, however extenuating the circumstances."

"Good heavens!" Lord Sefton exclaimed. "I can hardly imagine Wayne House without Gustave. Why, he has been with you for years!"

"Eight, to be precise!" the Marquis answered. "As a general rule, eight years is too long to keep a servant. He had grown lazy, careless, and he had also become dishonest!"

"Well, you astonish me!" Lord Alvanley remarked.

"You will therefore understand, General," the Marquis said, "that I shall be delighted to engage your Chef – if he is as good as you have just proclaimed!"

"I said better than Carême and I meant it!" the General replied.

"In which case I am prepared to bet quite a large sum that you are mistaken," Lord Sefton remarked.

"I think I must make this quite clear," the General said to the Marquis. "My Chef will come to you only on a temporary basis perhaps for one night or maybe two."

"I will employ him for only one night," the Marquis said, "just in case he is not as satisfactory as you seem to believe. Shall we say tomorrow? Tell him to call and see my secretary in the morning. I only hope the dinner will live up to your expectations."

He turned to go, but Lord Alvanley called after him:

"Hi, Wayne, you cannot leave like that! Not without giving me an invitation!"

"And me!" Lord Sefton interposed.

"You are both invited," the Marquis said, "and of course the General and Plymouth."

He turned to walk from the room without another word and the General stared after him reflectively.

He thought it poetic justice that the Marquis should provide some of the money which Araminta had to raise on Harry's behalf.

It was in fact quite an amusing thought and the General turned with a smile on his lips to Lord Alvanley.

"Well, that is something I never expected!" Lord Sefton remarked. "Wayne dispensing with Gustave and giving a dinner with an unknown Chef, without even requiring a reference or asking what it would cost him!"

"Why should it worry Wayne?" Lord Alvanley asked. "He is warm enough in the pocket. I only wish I had a penny for every sovereign he possesses!"

"If you had you would soon spend it, old chap!" Lord Plymouth laughed. "By the way, Uncle Alex, what does your paragon charge?"

The General hesitated.

"Twenty guineas!" he said.

"Twenty guineas!" Lord Alvanley cried. "Good God, that is too steep!"

"Not really," the General answered. "You know as well as I do that you gentlemen think nothing of spending ten guineas on one of the pretty Cyprians whom Madam Hayes provides in the Temple of Flora!"

He paused to add slyly:

"And I happen to know that Madam's so-called virgins are priced at twenty guineas!"

"Not much more than those money-grabbing vigilantes who haunted our camps in Portugal, eh General?" someone remarked.

The General ignored the interruption and continued speaking to Lord Alvanley.

"I consider the superlative delight of the dinner I envisage us enjoying tomorrow evening will exceed anything those ladies can offer!"

Lord Alvanley threw back his head and laughed.

"Dammit, Uncle Alex, but your argument is irrefutable and I do not dare to cross swords with you!"

"I hope not!" the General said solemnly.

"I suppose it will be an all-male party?" Lord Sefton interposed.

"Of course, you nit-wit!" Lord Alvanley replied. "What woman is capable of appreciating good food?"

"Is that why you never married?" his friend asked.

"It is one of the reasons," Lord Alvanley retorted, "the most important being that I could never afford a wife, and food is ultimately far more satisfying!"

"The French always say that it is the only thing you can do three times a day without getting bored!" Lord Plymouth remarked.

"All this talk of food is making me hungry," Lord Sefton said, "but I intend to be somewhat abstemious to-day and save myself for tomorrow evening."

He smiled at the General as he added:

"Do you think your wonder-Chef will give us thirty-six entrée such as Carême produced in Jappards for the Regent at the Royal Pavilion in Brighton?"

"I hope to Heaven not!" Lord Alvanley interposed before the General could speak. "I felt sick for a week afterwards! My stomach was blown out like 'Prinny's'!"

"You are getting more like him every day," Lord Sefton teased. "But you have to admit, fat though he may be, he is a damned good trencherman. I bet you he did not feel sick the next day and was ready for another thirty-six entrées the next night!"

"I will show you tomorrow night what I can do," Lord Alvanley promised. "Come on, Sefton, before you get too drunk to hold a pen, let us record our wagers in the betting-book."

They moved from the morning-room and the General looked after them with a faint smile.

Everything had gone exactly according to plan.

At the same time he could not help feeling that this idea of Araminta's might lead to trouble, although she seemed to have nothing to lose and twenty guineas was a great deal to gain.

'She will undoubtedly feel embarrassed at working in the kitchens of Wayne House,' he thought, 'but no-one will re-alise who she is and she is most unlikely to encounter the Marquis.'

The General was well aware that he had left the impression that the Chef he was proposing was a man. But noone would have thought for a moment that a Chef would be of any other sex.

Women cooks were considered very inferior and were unfashionable in London.

In the country some large mansions had women cooks they had employed for numbers of years, and who had risen from scullery-maid to kitchen-maid until they became the undisputed ruler of the back premises.

But in London the kitchens of the *Beau Monde* employed Chefs who, if they were not French, pretended to be, even assuming in some cases a foreign accent.

"Well at least I have done as Araminta asked me," the General said to himself as he settled in his favourite chair.

At the same time he felt uneasy.

CHAPTER TWO

"How are you getting on?" Caro asked.

Araminta looked up from the end of the table where she was surrounded by papers and had a writing-pad in front of her.

She put her quill pen back into the ink-pot before she answered:

"I have decided what I will cook for the Marquis and his guests. The difficulty is whether Hannah and I will be able to find all that is required at Covent Garden."

"I have always heard that it is the best market in the world," Caro said.

"Papa would not agree with you," Araminta smiled. "He thought the French markets superior in every way to anything we could provide in this country."

"It all depends on the menu," Caro said sensibly.

She picked up a piece of paper, saying:

"I have just found this amongst Papa's recipes, and it says that the Emperor Napoleon once had a dinner in Africa which featured tortoise broth, porcupine, gazelle, loin of wild boar, antelope cutlets and roast ostrich with pomegranate jelly!"

Araminta laughed.

"I am certainly not striving for anything as exotic as that! Have you all Papa's recipes there?"

"I brought them to London," Caro replied, "because I thought that if we had time you and I might put them together and make up a book."

"Caro, what a splendid idea!" Araminta exclaimed. "Perhaps we could get it published! Why did I not think of it?"

"I have considered it for some time," Caro said, "simply

33

because I remembered how Papa was always disparaging Mrs. Hannah's Glasse's books."

"He said that her '*Art of Cooking made Plain and Easy*' was certainly plain, and most of the dishes she recommended were easily avoided," Araminta laughed.

"If you want me to make the sotelties for you, I find her '*Complete Confectioner*' is quite useful."

"You make them far better than I do," Araminta said. "Papa always said your sugar baskets were the best he had ever eaten anywhere in the world."

Caro flushed with pleasure.

She was very lovely, but in a different way from her sister.

Both the sisters were fair, but Araminta had something almost spiritual about her small heart-shaped face, while Caro was always laughing and the dimples in her pink-and-white cheeks were as alluring as the twinkle in her eyes.

Both girls had aristocratic features with small straight noses, but Caro had a roguish expression which made everyone she met feel they wanted to smile with her.

Araminta was a replica of her mother, as she had looked when Sir Gilbert Sinclair had fallen head over heels in love with her at first sight. At the moment she had a frown on her smooth forehead as she said:

"It is very important that tomorrow evening's dinner should be a success, Caro, otherwise I may never have the chance of another engagement."

She sighed.

"And it is the only way we can find enough money .. to save Harry."

"I still cannot believe that the General has persuaded anyone to pay a person as much as twenty guineas to cook for one dinner!" Caro said with a note of awe in her voice.

"I too find it hard to believe," Araminta agreed. "Oh, Caro, suppose I .. fail?"

"You will not do that," Caro assured her confidently. "You know your cooking has always been superlative and I cannot believe that any of the recipes Papa brought back from abroad could possibly be rivalled anywhere in this country, with the exception, perhaps, of Carlton House."

"I think I have chosen all the dishes I do best," Araminta said, moving the pile of papers around her. "But look through Papa's collection, Caro, just in case there is something I have forgotten."

"I have been doing that while we have been sitting here," Caro replied, "and unless you want to give them something fantastic, I should just rely on doing the dishes which were always Papa's favourites."

"That is exactly what I have planned to do," Araminta said, "but according to Uncle Alex, the Marquis's Chef, whom he has just dismissed, was very good. I want to astonish the dinner party."

"What about the dishes they had at the 'Hell-Fire Club'?" Caro asked. "Papa went there when he was a young man and there is a menu here of one of the dinners."

"I am sure Mama would be shocked at your even having heard of a place as wicked as the 'Hell-Fire Club'."

"Or perhaps you would prefer some of the Roman dishes about which Papa made special notes?" Caro suggested with a teasing note in her voice. "There was the Emperor Heliogabalus for instance, who had six hundred ostriches killed so that he could cook the heads and eat the brains."

"It sounds horrible and very cruel!" Araminta exclaimed.

"He also considered camels' feet to be a great delicacy," Caro continued. "But according to Papa, the rich Romans were gastronomic monomaniacs, who spent enormous fortunes on every meal."

"Personally I prefer to read about the Greeks," Araminta said. "Papa always told me that they invented sauces and there were the seven Sages of the Kitchen."

"Yes, I remember Papa saying that," Caro said, "and there was one who lived in Corinth who made a 'conger eel dish fit for the gods'."

She made a little grimace.

"I cannot say I am anxious to eat a conger eel."

"Nor am I," Araminta agreed, "and that is why the Marquis will have salmon tomorrow night."

"Oh, not salmon!" Caro exclaimed. "You cannot have anything so banal! Papa said that at every English dinner to which he was invited he was given Mulligatawny soup, salmon, and saddle of mutton!"

"Salmon from the Thames is really the only fish that I can be certain will be fresh," Araminta said firmly.

It was true, they both knew, that except for salmon, the fish brought into the City, even by the specially designed and very speedy land-carriages, was invariably stale by the time it reached the market.

The meat too came regularly from remote districts, but it arrived alive – 'on the hoof'.

No matter how rancid it became afterwards in the market and cook-shops, it was fresh when it reached London.

Poultry also came frequently but slowly on foot from the flat fields of Norfolk and Suffolk.

Araminta was well aware that the success of her dinner would rest primarily on the quality of the food before she cooked it.

Fortunately Hannah, their old maid, who had been with them since their mother first married, knew exactly what was required.

Araminta had already told her they must set out very early the next morning for Covent Garden to do the shopping.

Hannah was at first horrified not only that Araminta should demean herself by being paid for her cooking, but also that it should be done in a strange gentleman's house.

"I can't think what your mother'll say about it when she hears!" she remarked sourly.

"You must not tell her! Please Hannah, do not breathe a word to Mama at the moment!" Araminta begged. "There is no point in worrying her unnecessarily, and you know how upset she will be when she learns that Harry is in debt."

Fortunately Hannah adored Harry.

He was her favourite of the family, and she would have lain down on the floor at any time to let him walk over her should he wish to do so.

She was therefore prepared to say nothing and not only to take Araminta to Covent Garden, but also to help prepare

36

many of the dishes before they were taken to Wayne House.

This Araminta had discussed with the General when he had come immediately after luncheon to tell her that her idea had succeeded.

She also learnt that her employer was to be none other than the Marquis of Wayne, who would pay her the incredible sum of twenty guineas for cooking one meal.

Fortunately Lady Sinclair was lying down and the two sisters sat in the drawing-room listening wide-eyed while the General explained how he had conducted his campaign in White's Club.

"Uncle Alex, you are a genius!" Araminta exclaimed. "But twenty guineas! I feel ashamed at the thought of accepting so much money."

"You will earn it, my dear," the General said dryly.

"But from the Marquis of Wayne!" Araminta exclaimed. "Supposing he .. finds out who I .. am?"

"It is most important that he should not do so," the General said, "and I am certain you have already decided not to use your own name."

"Indeed I have," Araminta answered. "I thought I would be French and call myself Mademoiselle Bouvais. It was the name of our dear old Chef, who taught me everything I know."

"May I tactfully suggest," the General asked, "that you do not look in the least French?"

"You had much better be Miss Bouvais," Caro said. "After all, if pressed you can say you had a French father and an English mother."

"Papa always said that if one was going to tell a lie, then it should be a good one!" Araminta smiled, "and one must never make it too elaborate."

"Then it had best be Miss Bouvais," the General remarked.

"I am hoping to keep the Marquis from knowing that I am a woman until after he has eaten his dinner," Araminta said. "Would that be possible?"

"You think it would prejudice his appreciation of your culinary powers?" the General asked.

"You know what men are like," Araminta answered scornfully. "They will never admit a woman can cook as well as a man. In fact Papa only allowed that I was a superlative cook because I had a superlative teacher in old Bouvais!'

The General laughed.

"I am afraid women will never reach equality with the superior male!"

"Why should they want to?" Araminta asked indifferently. "But as we wish the Marquis to feel his twenty guineas has been well spent, it would be advisable for him to think that I am a male replacement for the Chef he has dismissed."

They decided that the General should call at Wayne House on the way home.

He promised to see the Marquis's secretary, whose name he told Araminta was Major Brownlow, and explain that the chef he was recommending would not arrive until the afternoon.

"You have a chance of escaping detection," he said, "because Major Brownlow lost a leg when he was in the Peninsula."

"Oh, poor man!" Araminta exclaimed.

"He was a very gallant officer," the General went on, "one of the best under my command. I have always been grateful to Wayne for employing him, otherwise he might have found life very difficult."

"What you are telling me," Araminta said, "is that it is very unlikely that Major Brownlow will descend to the kitchen quarters to interview me."

"I think, if you are clever," the General replied, "you can avoid meeting him, at any rate until the dinner is over. If he sends for you, make the excuse that the pot might boil over!"

Araminta clapped her hands together.

"Uncle Alex, you are a born intriguer! I only hope I do not disgrace you."

"You will never do that, my dear," the General said fondly, "and if this mad escapade succeeds I shall in fact be very proud of you!"

"It has to succeed!" Caro said firmly. "You will find

Uncle Alex, that after tomorrow night you will be inundated with requests for Araminta's services."

"I hope so," the General said seriously.

He had told Araminta that he had seen the Marquis before he left White's Club and discovered that he intended having no more than ten guests to dinner.

"I am inviting only the gourmets, General," the Marquis said. "You have issued a challenge and I am determined to have adjudicators who have knowledge of what they are judging."

"You do not frighten me, Wayne," the General answered. "I am prepared to back my choice against all-comers."

"You are very confident," the Marquis said mockingly.

The General had the impression that His Lordship was sure that the dinner would not be a success.

He did not of course mention this to Araminta, but as he looked at the two young girls sitting beside him he wondered if in fact the battle ahead had not already been lost.

Then he remembered some of the delicious food he had consumed at their home in Bedfordshire and told himself that, if Araminta now cooked as well as she had then, it would be impossible for anyone to find fault with her cuisine.

At the same time when he left Russell Square he was still uneasy.

Caro was looking through her father's papers.

Sir Gilbert Sinclair had travelled a great deal before he married, and during the war he had been first in Italy, then France, Spain, Portugal and finally Brussels.

Even after he was wounded he had still been interested in food and any dish which took his fancy was always meticulously written down and added to his collection of recipes.

"Here is a good one!" Caro exclaimed. "Why not try to do this? It is called 'The Shield of Minerva' and was invented by Vitellius who, according to Papa, was a great Roman gastronome."

She was obviously teasing and Araminta was not listening, but Caro went on:

"It consists of a mixture of the liver of the parrot fish,

the brains of the peacock and the pheasant, the tongues of flamingos and the entrails of lampreys!'

The door opened and Harry came in.

He had already been told of the General's success in finding a host to ask for Araminta's services and had expressed his disapproval very forcefully at the idea of her going to the house of the Marquis of Wayne.

"I could hardly refuse his offer, Harry," the General said.

"I know that, Sir, but if it ever becomes known that I have encouraged my sister to earn money in order to pay my debts I would never be able to hold my head up in public again."

"No-one will know, Harry, I promise you," Araminta said.

But she knew he was not convinced, and now as he entered the room she looked up sharply and felt her heart drop a little at the expression on his face.

"What is it?" she asked.

Harry sat down on a chair by the table.

"I have just been to White's."

Neither of the girls spoke and after a moment he went on:

"They are laying bets on this dinner and, as far as I can make out, if it is a success tomorrow night, the Marquis intends giving a second party the following evening."

For a moment there was a look of consternation on Araminta's face then she said:

"That will be £42! Harry, just think of it .. forty guineas!"

Harry gave a little groan.

"I know it is a lot of money," he said, "but I have no right to let you do this."

"No-one is likely to find out," Araminta told him, "and if only we had a little more time I could make enough so that we would not have to ask Mama for her engagement ring."

"I suppose I could place a bet on you," Harry said tentatively.

Araminta gave a little cry.

"Do not dare! You have promised, Harry, that you will never gamble again. If you break your promise I will never forgive you – never!"

She spoke so violently that Harry said quickly:

"It is all right, Araminta. I gave you my promise, and I swear I will not break it. I am very grateful to you, I really am. It is only that I feel so worried."

"We all do," Caro said. "But I cannot help feeling that Papa would be rather amused by it all."

. . . .

The following morning Araminta knew that her father would not have been amused but extremely interested at the food she found in the market.

It was well known that as the market was expensive, the majority of people bought their food from stalls and barrows.

Araminta and Hannah went first to the meat and poultry market at Newgate.

It was estimated that at the end of the last century over a hundred thousand head of cattle came annually to the London markets by road.

Never had Araminta seen so much beef, mutton, veal and venison, or so many hares, hens, ducks and geese.

She hesitated over some fat turkeys and tender young guinea fowl, but the menu on which she decided had a special recipe for stuffing pigeons with foie gras, chestnuts, and olives and she decided not to make a change.

There were also swans for sale and those, Araminta knew, were an exotic dish that many people considered a great delicacy.

But they were often tough and the Marquis himself, she thought, might have a dislike of them.

She decided to keep to the simple and in some ways ordinary fish and poultry, but to prepare them in the French manner which made each dish taste so delicious that it would be unlike anything most Englishmen were ever fortunate enough to encounter.

There was a big variety at Newgate Market, but much more colour to the piles of fruit and vegetables at Covent Garden.

While Araminta stared wide-eyed and delighted by everything, Hannah sniffed disparagingly. She had grumbled about the food in London ever since they had left home.

Cabbages, radishes and spinach which grew round the City, she thought, were so impregnated with smoke from the sea-coal which filled the atmosphere that they had a disagreeable taste.

However, she believed that asparagus was exempt and it was so cheap and plentiful she was prepared to let Araminta buy a lot of it.

Fruit, Hannah was convinced, was cleaned of dust with spittle!

She had also been told, although goodness knows by whom, that town cows were kept in dark, very crowded, filthy conditions, and she had, ever since they arrived from the country, refused to buy milk from the milk-maids who carried open cans of milk on their heads and sold it from door to door.

She had, however, to admit that the sauces Araminta intended to make required cream, and finally they found some which the vendor swore came direct from a farm, and was a rich yellow.

Araminta purchased, too, the best butter which came by sea from East Anglia and eggs which were alleged to have been laid the day before.

"His Lordship is certain to have all these things sent to London from his country estate," Hannah said.

"I dare not risk being short of eggs and cream," Araminta replied. "I will want three pints for the syllabub alone."

There was a variety of cheeses which took her breath away and she had great difficulty in making a choice between Cheshire, Gloucester, Wiltshire, Cheddar and Stilton.

At Leadenhall Market they found the salmon Araminta wanted – a princeling which the vendor swore had come from the river that very morning.

She also found the cockles, shrimps, mussels and oysters she required for sauces.

They drove home in a hackney carriage piled high with their purchases and as soon as they reached the house in Russell Square, Araminta and Hannah set to work.

It was fortunate that Lady Sinclair, tired after the journey to London, had decided to spend the day in bed.

"I am so sorry for you, Mama," Araminta said when she went to her mother's bed-room.

At the same time she was aware that it could not have been better for their plans that Lady Sinclair was confined to her room. She would in consequence have no idea of what was going on downstairs in the basement kitchen.

Araminta and Hannah had decided that everything possible would be prepared before she left the house.

This meant there would only be the final heating and decorating to be done when she reached the Marquis's kitchen, and the sauces to mix which no-one could do but herself.

Caro had been at work from the time they left for Covent Garden preparing the sotelties at which she was an expert.

Sotelties were delicacies made of sugar, fashioned into a fanciful shape, which made an artistic end to a meal.

It had amused Sir Gilbert to describe to his daughter some famous sotelties he had discovered in ancient books on great French and English entertainments.

He had read to his daughters about those that had distinguished the table of Henry V when he brought home his French bride Catherine, one of them representing a pelican sitting on its nest and another showing St. Catherine surrounded by angels.

"They must have been too good to eat," Caro said when she was a small girl.

"And I should imagine that after they had been painted, gilded and fashioned by dirty fingers they would very likely taste unpleasant!" Sir Gilbert had remarked dryly.

At the same time sotelties could be very intriguing.

Araminta found that Caro was making a big basket of sugar which was decorated with pink roses and filled with sugar coated strawberries, crystallized violets and *petit fours* of marzipan.

She had also prepared an original pudding in the shape of a hedgehog, made from cream, eggs, sugar, orange-flower water, canary and hartshorn.

When it was moulded into the right shape it was stuck with almond quills and had two blackcurrant eyes.

"That is really a child's dish," Araminta laughed.

43

"And what are these gentlemen but children?" Hannah sniffed. "Stuffing their bellies with good food and never a thought for those as prepares it!"

"I do not wish the Marquis to give me 'a thought'," Araminta replied.

She had already planned that Hannah would go with her in a hackney carriage to Wayne House carrying with great care all the dishes which were ready.

Araminta would take also with her the bill for their purchases which came in her eyes, to an astronomical sum.

"I hope His Lordship will not think it too much," she murmured when she saw what they had spent.

"If he wants good food he has to pay for it!" Hannah said practically. "And mind you get your own wages, Miss Araminta, before you leave. It'd be just like you to forget them."

"I will not forget," Araminta answered. "We are doing this for Harry, Hannah, and everything depends upon it."

Harry had offered to take Araminta to Wayne House, but although she thanked him for the suggestion she thought it too dangerous.

"If anyone should see us together they might become suspicious," she said. "Hannah will go with me."

"And will she return with you?"

"Of course," Araminta answered.

He was satisfied and asked no more questions, but as it happened, Araminta had no intention of keeping Hannah out so late.

She was old and had already had a hard day, having risen early and worked with her in the kitchen, besides being continually in attendance on Lady Sinclair.

Her mother had said to Araminta when she went to her room before setting out to Wayne House:

"Tomorrow, darling, we must start buying your new gowns."

"There is no hurry, Mama," Araminta replied, "and I think it would be wise to settle ourselves in the house first, and look around before we actually spend any money."

"You are so practical, dearest," Lady Sinclair smiled.

"I have to be," Araminta answered.

She had kissed her mother and said:

"Do not worry about anything, Mama. Just rest. It has been very tiring for you packing up and coming to London."

"You are all so good to me. But I do miss your father," Lady Sinclair sighed.

"Yes, of course you do," Araminta answered. "So go to sleep and dream about him."

"I always try to," Lady Sinclair replied simply.

Araminta had left her mother's room, hurriedly put on a dark cape over her simple gown and gone outside to find Hannah already waiting in a hackney carriage.

"Look after Mama," she said to Caro as she stepped in, "and do not let her suspect for a moment that I am not at home."

"You can leave everything to me," Caro replied.

She waved as the carriage drove away with Araminta and Hannah holding the most fragile dishes carefully on their laps.

Araminta had expected Wayne House to be impressive, but not so big, nor so attractive as it actually was.

Situated in Park Lane, it was a very fine example of early Georgian architecture and had been built by the Marquis's grandfather early in the previous century.

The porticoed front door was Grecian, and behind the house there was a garden which contained large trees and a profusion of flowering shrubs.

The lilacs, syringa and rhododendrons made Araminta for a moment feel homesick for the country.

Then as the hackney carriage drove to the side door, she remembered that she was a servant employed by the owner of the house.

The kitchen, as she had expected, was in the basement, and she went down the stone steps to ring a bell which brought a boot-boy, in his shirt sleeves, but wearing a striped waistcoat with silver buttons, to the door.

Although Araminta was wearing a plain cloak with its hood over her fair hair he stared at her in astonishment.

"I am the new Chef," Araminta said crisply. "I will be most obliged if you will carry in from the hackney carriage the food I have brought with me."

45

The boy gaped at her. Then, as if he had lost his tongue in his astonishment, he ran up the steps to obey her command.

Araminta walked down the stone-flagged passage to the kitchen.

As she entered she was relieved to see that it was in fact furnished with the latest equipment.

She had been rather afraid, from all she had heard of old-fashioned and often dirty kitchens, that the Marquis, being unmarried, would not have provided his Chef with the latest 'Rumford Stove'.

This invention by an American of Massachusetts had revolutionised methods of cooking and utilised heat to greater advantage.

The Regent had set a high standard of kitchen reform with the magnificent and exquisitely decorated kitchens he had installed at the Royal Pavilion in Brighton.

Araminta thought as she looked around her that she might have guessed that anyone as distinguished as the Marquis of Wayne would wish to follow His Royal Highness's example.

At the back of her mind she had, as she journeyed towards Wayne House, been nervous in case she would find frying-pans, griddles and kettles swinging from chains over an open fire, various kinds of spits for roasting meat and a terrifyingly complicated machine on three legs which toasted meat.

Now she laughed at herself for having been apprehensive. In fact the Marquis's kitchen was not only as light and airy as a basement room could ever be, but it was also undeniably clean.

She had, however, very little time to inspect her surroundings before she became aware that the kitchen was filling up with a varying collection of servants, all staring at her in astonishment.

There were several women in enveloping white aprons and mob-caps who she knew were kitchen and scullery-maids.

There were two boys like the one she had sent to the hackney carriage and two elderly males whom she suspected of being the 'odd-job' men.

They brought in the coal, stoked the stove, cleaned the boots and helped the knife-boy grind the knives.

Her mother had often explained to her the very complicated hierarchy of a great household, but Araminta had never come in contact with it until now.

She saw several very tall, good-looking young men join the others and was aware from their smart claret and gold livery that they were footmen.

It seemed to Araminta that everyone was uncomfortably silent, so at last she smiled and said pleasantly:

"Good-afternoon! I am Bouvais – the new Chef!"

"The Chef?"

The words were repeated almost like a cry. Then, before anyone could reply, a deep authoritative voice asked:

"What's going on here?"

There was no doubt that the elderly man with white hair and the pontifical expression of an Archbishop was the Butler.

The servants divided for him to pass through them and he walked towards Araminta looking, if anything, more surprised than they had been.

"*You* are the new Chef?" he enquired. "It's impossible!"

"It is nevertheless a fact!" Araminta answered. "And I think you must be the Butler."

"I'm Mr. Henson."

"And I am Miss Bouvais!"

With an effort the Butler held out his hand.

"I'm pleased to meet you, Miss Bouvais, but I'll not disguise the fact that you're a surprise."

"I expected that I would be," Araminta answered, "and because you are all so astonished, may I ask a great favour?"

They all waited, round-eyed, staring at her.

"Because I want His Lordship to enjoy his dinner tonight without being prejudiced," Araminta said, "would you be very kind and not let him be aware that a woman is doing the cooking until the dinner is over?"

47

She saw a look of uncertainty come into the Butler's face and added quickly:

"I would not ask you to lie, of course; but it is unlikely, I feel, that His Lordship will enquire as to whether the Chef is male or female."

She paused, realising her point had been taken by those listening.

"And if Major Brownlow should ask to see me, I thought it would be possible for you to say that Chef could not come upstairs at that particular moment."

She spoke so earnestly, her grey eyes pleading for understanding, and she looked so young as she did so, that quite unexpectedly the Butler began to laugh.

"I see, Miss Bouvais," he said, "that you intend to give His Lordship a shock when he learns the truth."

"Why not, Mr. Henson?" Araminta asked, "And I promise you that this woman, at any rate, cooks just as well as any man!"

"I only hope you're right, Miss Bouvais," the Butler remarked.

And she knew that whatever Mr. Henson decreed would be scrupulously observed by the others.

The boy whom Araminta had sent to the hackney carriage appeared carrying a large dish on which reposed the hedgehog.

"You have prepared some of the food already?" the Butler enquired.

"Quite a lot of it," Araminta answered. "I was unable to come here until now, as I believe Major Brownlow was informed."

"Yes, he was," the Butler agreed.

"Then perhaps someone else could help bring in the food in the carriage outside?" Araminta suggested.

The Butler snapped his fingers and the boys who had been gaping and two of the footmen hurried to obey his orders.

Soon the big table in the middle of the kitchen was full and Araminta, having taken off her cloak, was instructing the kitchen-maids.

"There is a cool larder somewhere, I expect?" she asked.

"Yes, Miss," one of the maids answered and opened a door at the end of the kitchen.

It was the sort of larder which Araminta had hoped to find, with cool marble slabs. There were big pans of cream and quite a collection of joints of beef, legs of lamb and trussed chickens.

Several of the dishes Araminta had brought with her were arranged on the empty slabs. Then she went back to the kitchen.

The Butler and the servants who were not helping her were staring at the salmon which she and Hannah had purchased during the morning.

"Is that salmon?" the Butler asked.

"It is!" Araminta agreed.

"And covered with pastry?"

"As you see!"

"I've never seen the like of that before!"

"It is the Russian way of cooking fish," Araminta informed him.

She did not explain that her father had brought back the recipe on one of his travels, and that it was in fact one of his favourite dishes.

She knew that the manner in which it was prepared, the flesh being mixed with a very special sauce, then moulded back into shape, covered with finely chopped mushrooms, and finally encased with light pastry, would be an unusual presentation, even at the Marquis's table.

The same applied to every other dish which Araminta had chosen.

Mutton, so young it might almost have been lamb, was to be stuffed with cockles and herrings and have a watercress sauce.

Apples Araminta intended to chop finely and mix with horse-radish and cream for a delicious fruity sauce to be eaten with the meat.

The *Côtelettes d'agneau Maintenon* which had originally been invented in honour of Madame de Maintenon were, she knew, so tender and delicious that they were worthy of the *grands seigneurs* who once enjoyed them.

She set to work arranging her dishes in the order in which

49

she would need them. Then she prepared the sauces which would go with them.

Afterwards she decorated some dishes with grapes, tomatoes, oranges, lemons, pimentos, green olives and celery, others were garlanded with green leaves and the heads of flowers.

"I've never see'd flowers on a dish before!" one of the kitchen-maids exclaimed.

"You see how pretty they look! Let us encircle this pudding just with pink roses and the chocolate mousse with white," Araminta suggested.

They had been working for about an hour-and-a-half when the maids informed Araminta that it was time for their meal.

"We eats early, Miss," one said. "That gives us time to attend to His Lordship and we has supper afore we goes to bed."

Araminta went with them into the servants' hall where there was all the food that would have made her father laugh and which he had tried to avoid all his life.

There were huge joints of red beef, coarsely cooked brawns, hams sliced thickly, chickens which, Araminta knew, the men-servants thought of as 'women's fare', and heavy suet-puddings stuffed with sultanas and currants, or swimming in jams.

There was also newly baked bread, pats of golden butter, and ale for everyone who wanted it.

The Butler sat at one end of the table, Araminta was invited to take the other end. The housekeeper, she learnt, ate with the two head housemaids in her own sitting-room.

The servants started to eat greedily and noisily, but Araminta, after managing to consume a small amount of chicken and a slice of ox-tongue, realised she was too anxious to be hungry.

"I hope you will excuse me," she said tentatively, "but I would like to get on with the sauces."

"We won't keep you, Miss Bouvais," the Butler said. "We know how determined you are to surprise the Master this evening and, mark my words, he'll get a surprise!"

Araminta smiled at him and went back to the kitchen.

There was still a lot to do, she thought, and walked into the larder to look at the dishes that she had left on the cold slab.

Then she gave an exclamation of annoyance.

Up on the slab, licking at a bowl containing eggs and cream, was a large ginger cat!

"Shoo! Shoo! Go away!" Araminta exclaimed.

The cat sprang onto the floor as she hastily looked to see what damage had been done.

The bowl had contained the eggs and cream which were the foundation of the *crème brûlée*. Araminta had intended to sprinkle it with sugar and place it under a hot grill until the coating of sugar had melted into a sheet of golden brown caramel with the consistency of toffee.

Now it would have to be thrown away, and there was no time in which to make another.

She put the bowl down on the floor and said to the cat who was glowering at her in a corner:

"Come on then. If you want to make a pig of yourself you might as well finish this off. It will at least prevent you from touching anything else!"

The cat, who was fat and obviously greedy, crept towards the bowl and started to lick up the eggs and cream mixture with relish.

"That is an extremely expensive dish for a cat!" Araminta went on. "It also makes me short on my menu, so I ought to be very angry with you!"

She thought however that the sotelties which Caro had made looked so pretty that the dinner guests were unlikely to be interested in anything else.

As well as the huge hedgehog and the sugar baskets, there were 'French Fish-Ponds' and 'Floating Islands' which her father had found in 17th century cookery books.

'I wish we had had more time,' Araminta thought, 'then Caro and I could have made a Grecian Temple like the one we once made on Papa's birthday, or even a Castle with a battle taking place around it.'

She re-arranged the dishes knowing that the *crème*

brûlée would not be missed. Then she looked down at the cat thinking she must move it out of the larder before it did any more harm.

She stared!

Beside the bowl of *crème brûlée* the ginger cat was lying on its side.

'How could it have fallen asleep so quickly?' Araminta wondered.

Even as she asked herself the question she knew that something was wrong!

She bent down to touch the cat. Its body was warm but its lips were drawn back in a strange way from its teeth. The green eyes which had glowed at her had an expression in them which Araminta had seen before.

Incredibly – shockingly – the ginger cat was dead!

She knelt beside it for some seconds. Then she looked at the half-empty bowl and a terrible suspicion came into her mind.

She did not know why, but somehow she knew that the bowl of eggs and cream she had prepared for the *crème brûlée* had been poisoned!

But by whom? And why?

For a moment it was difficult for Araminta to think clearly.

She only knew one thing – that if anyone at the dinner-party had died in the same manner as the cat, it was quite obvious who would be suspected of being implicated in the crime!

As if she was seeing a melodrama unfold before her eyes, Araminta was aware of how significant it would appear that Harry's sister should have cooked a meal after which the host had died.

And if he had done so, would it not be obvious that she had wished to be rid of the Marquis because of her brother's debt?

It all seemed to flash through her mind, even as she told herself that the whole thing was preposterous and could not really have happened.

But there, undeniably, beside her lay the dead cat – a cat who had been alive and greedy only a few minutes ago.

Araminta rose to her feet.

Whatever happened, she thought, no-one in the household must be aware of the cat's fate.

They would talk and any suggestion of there being poison in the larder would cause an immediate commotion.

There was also no chance of her running away to avoid an unpleasant situation, because that would involve the General.

She looked around the larder frantically.

Could anything else have been poisoned?

To insert poison into the hedgehog, the sugar baskets, the Floating Islands or the French Fish-ponds, would be to disturb their appearance.

But everything looked exactly as it had when she had put them on the marble slab.

Only the *crème brûlée* had been left unfinished and it had therefore been easy to insert poison into it.

No-one could possibly have suspected that anything had been added to the bowl, if it had not attracted the ginger cat.

Araminta felt very frightened but she knew she had to do something quickly.

The question was . . what?

The first thing was to get rid of the dead cat.

She picked it up and realised it was stiffening in a manner which recalled all too clearly the death of her own cat two years ago.

It had been kinder, her mother had said, to put Flumbo to sleep, and the gardener had given him rat poison which had worked instantly.

Old Flumbo, when he was dead, looked very like the ginger cat which Araminta now held in her arms.

'It is poisoned!' she thought. 'I am sure it is!'

She carried the cat into the scullery which opened out into the larder and found a cupboard underneath a sink. She put the cat inside it and shut the door.

She went back to the larder and picked up the bowl. Quickly she threw away the contents and washed it out.

She was drying it when one of the kitchen-maids came into the scullery.

53

"I came to see if I could help, Miss," she said.

"Thank you," Araminta answered. "There is still quite a lot to be done."

"What was in that bowl?" the girl asked curiously, looking at the bowl in Araminta's hands.

"It was to have been a *crème brûlée*," Araminta explained, "but the ingredients curdled, so I threw them away."

"That's a real pity, Miss, because *crème brûlée* is one of His Lordship's favourite dishes. *Monsieur* Gustave always made it for him once or twice a week."

Araminta put the bowl down before she asked:

"Has Monsieur Gustave left the house?"

"Oh, yes, Miss. He went yesterday – and very angry he was too!"

"And he has not returned since?" Araminta asked.

"Funny you should say that, Miss. Henry, that's one of the footmen, was saying just now as how he'd be back some time this afternoon for a piece of his luggage as he'd left behind."

"Where was the luggage?" Araminta asked.

"In the passage, Miss, waiting for *Monsieur* Gustave to fetch it."

"Was it there when I arrived?" Araminta enquired.

"Yes, Miss. I sees it just afore Jim went to answer your knock on the door."

Araminta moved towards the kitchen.

"Will you look and see if it is still there?"

The kitchen-maid looked surprised, but she had been taught not to ask questions of senior servants.

She went to the kitchen door and returned after a moment to say:

"It's gone, Miss! *Monsieur* Gustave must have come for it when we were in the hall."

Araminta said nothing.

She knew now who had poisoned the *crème brûlée*. Gustave was well aware that given a choice of dishes it was the one his Master was likely to prefer.

She could not help thinking with a little shudder how

inevitably she would have been accused of poisoning the Marquis.

Even if it had not killed him as it had the ginger cat, how could she have proclaimed her innocence and averred that she was not directly interested in the Marquis's death?

She felt for a moment quite faint at the thought of what a scandal it would have caused.

She might have been taken to the Old Bailey, Harry would have been involved and the general assumption that he had persuaded his sister to help pay off his debt would have brought disgrace to the whole family.

'It is all right,' she tried to comfort herself as she fought against an encroaching dizziness. 'You are saved!'

Saved because a ginger cat was greedy!

CHAPTER THREE

"You are a strange man, My Lord!"

The Marquis of Wayne smiled at the speaker and thought, as he had often thought before, that she looked extremely alluring.

Her body was perfect, her breasts high and her waist very small.

"In what way?" he asked.

Harriette Wilson pondered a moment before she replied:

"It is difficult to put into words, but there is always a barrier between us even in our most intimate moments. I have the feeling that it is not especially because of deficiencies that it is erected."

"If there is a barrier," the Marquis replied, "then I assure you that it exists for everyone and has nothing to do with you personally."

"I rather suspected that," Harriette replied, "and I have been wondering what it is! Why do you keep us all – perhaps the world itself – at arm's length?"

"Do I do that?" the Marquis enquired.

But the manner in which he spoke told Harriette that he was well aware that what she said was the truth.

"No woman," she said aloud, "would consider you anything but the most attractive, the most satisfying and the most experienced lover."

"Thank you, Harriette," the Marquis answered. "That, coming from an expert in the art of love is, I assure you, a compliment which I value highly!"

"I wonder . ." Harriette said reflectively.

Her eyes were dancing with amusement and her attractive, provocative red lips were curved in a little smile.

"I have a feeling," she went on after a moment, "that

there is something inconsistent behind that façade of all-conquering superiority."

The Marquis did not reply and she continued:

"I understand what your friends – or should I say your enemies? – mean when they say you are insufferably sure of yourself. Sometimes I wonder if in your heart you are as autocratically omnipotent as you choose to appear."

"You are putting me under a microscope, Harriette, and I do not like it!" the Marquis said sharply. "Also, as you are well aware, I never talk about myself."

"That is surprisingly true," Harriette remarked, "and I think you are the only man of my acquaintance who is not absorbedly interested in a discussion concerning himself."

"I am glad to be the exception – now let us talk about you."

The Marquis put his arms around her and drew her close to him, but when he would have kissed her Harriette turned her lips away.

"I want to know the truth," she pouted. "Why can you not be as easy to understand as all the other men who have made love to me?"

"Perhaps I prefer to keep you guessing!" the Marquis laughed.

Now, masterfully, he pulled her little pointed chin round with his long fingers and his mouth held hers captive.

He had intended to take Harriette Wilson driving in his new High-Perch Phaeton, but as it was raining they had employed the afternoon in a more amusing and far more intimate manner.

Harriette was one of the best-known personalities in London.

She had been born of quite respectable parents; she was not only extremely pretty and distinguished-looking but also highly intelligent.

She spoke French fluently and had an excellent taste in literature.

One of her first lovers, the Honourable Frederick Lamb, son of Lord Melbourne, had helped her to develop her natural gifts and had read Shakespeare, Virgil, Milton and Johnson aloud to her.

57

Harriette had been seduced at the age of fifteen by Lord Craven and he had been followed by a succession of noble lovers.

She was extremely fastidious and only recently had been very elusive when the Duke of Wellington had paid £100 to a Mrs. Porter for an introduction to her.

Mrs. Porter had become rich by making the preliminary arrangements when aristocrats desired to meet beautiful young women of doubtful virtue.

The introduction between the Duke and Harriette had finally been arranged, but on one occasion when they met she treated him most unkindly.

White's Club had been regaled with the story of how the great commander had called at her house by arrangement, only to be sent away by the Duke of Argyle.

Leaning out of a window and wearing one of Harriette's nightcaps, he pretended to be her *duenna* who was too deaf and too blind to understand the identity of her distinguished caller.

Harriette had wickedly described to the Marquis how Wellington had pulled off his hat and dripping wet, the rain trickling down his nose, had shouted at Argyle:

"You old idiot, do you not know me now?"

"Lord Sir," Argyle quavered, "I can't give no guess!"

She laughed and added:

"After all, two's company in bed!"

But for all her mischievous ways, Harriette had no intention of playing hard-to-get where the Marquis was concerned.

She had in fact pursued him for some time, knowing that while there were dozens of young men only too anxious to be her lover, the Marquis, while always treating her with politeness, had never made a single advance in her direction.

There was something about him which attracted her more than she liked to admit.

It was not, she told herself, his extreme good looks, although he was indeed as handsome as Lord Ponsonby with whom she had been in love for some years.

It was not his wealth; for Harriette had plenty of rich men willing to provide her with anything she required.

And it was not his reputation with horses, swords or pistols that she found alluring.

She came to the conclusion ultimately that it was two things. First his outstanding good manners, for her own manners were in fact as attractive as her appearance – and secondly an indescribable air of aloofness.

Having had so many men at her feet, Harriette, like all women, was ready to be beguiled by someone different and there was no doubt the Marquis was that!

As Harriette's lovers all seemed to belong to White's Club she knew the latest scandal before it reached the Mayfair salons, and also the estimation men had for each other.

Lord Alvanley, for whom Harriette had a warm affection and friendship, Lord Yarmouth and Lord Worcester, all talked about the Marquis.

Long before she actually met him, Harriette knew that he intrigued her and there was something about him that set him apart from his friends.

And yet, even when she had finally lured him into her bed, she found that unlike her other lovers, the man behind the fascinating façade eluded her.

Harriette was clever enough to realise there was something in the Marquis that was out of reach and frank enough with herself to acknowledge that, like a will o' the wisp, it was very unlikely she would ever capture it.

In the meantime she enjoyed being in the Marquis's company and found that not only was he an irresistible lover but that she also enjoyed his mind.

He was witty, he was knowledgeable, and her only complaint was that the Marquis would not spend as much time with her as she would have wished.

Nevertheless Harriette had learnt in a hard school to be grateful for what she had and not to cry for the moon.

She and her sisters, Amy and Sophia, had deliberately chosen their particular way of life and had formed what one member of White's had called 'an unholy Trinity!'

Sophia, who was Harriette's younger sister, had first been led astray by Lord Deerhurst and was afterwards kept by Lord Berwick.

She very cleverly persuaded him to marry her and from an imposing family mansion in Grosvenor Square she had, for the last four years, patronised her two sisters.

Amy, having begun her career by making an unhappy marriage, was now back 'on the town', and could be seen in a box at the Opera surrounded by all the fashionable Bucks. She had in fact often been squired by Beau Brummell.

But Harriette was undoubtedly the most attractive of the sisters and there was no-one in the whole of London to rival either her looks or her charm.

"It is typical," someone said sourly at White's, "that Wayne with his usual devil's luck should now have captivated Harriette. She was becoming interested in me until he came along!"

"There is no use in trying to rival Wayne, my dear fellow," one of his friends replied. "You know as well as I do that he is always first past the winning-post, and in at every kill."

"I would give a thousand pounds to see him get a good set-down," the first speaker said bitterly.

There was a note in his voice which revealed all too clearly that he knew it was a forlorn hope.

The Marquis, having kissed Harriette to his satisfaction, released her and said:

"I must leave you now. The Regent is coming to dinner to-night and so I must return home."

"Are you giving a large party?" Harriette asked.

"Only about twenty," the Marquis replied. "I have a new Chef and I want to watch the Prince's face when he realises that he is better than Carême."

"Is that possible?" Harriette enquired.

"It is – but I did not believe it myself until last night," the Marquis admitted.

"What happened last night?" Harriette enquired curiously.

"General Bracknell announced in the Club that he had a

Chef who was better than Carême," the Marquis said.

He smiled before he went on:

"It was a challenge I could not resist, having believed that Carême had no equal, in this country at any rate."

"That is what I had always heard," Harriette agreed.

"We were mistaken," the Marquis said. "There is a man called Bouvais who can, without exception, cook better than any Chef I have ever known."

"How can you be so unkind as to not include me in your party this evening?" Harriette asked.

"It is solely for gourmets, my dear," the Marquis replied, "and food is not, I think, one of your vices, or should I say virtues?"

"I enjoy good food!" Harriette said positively.

"There is a difference between the excellent food such as you have offered me here and the food with which I intend to infuriate the Regent this evening."

"You are making me curious and a little envious," Harriette protested.

"I will invite you to dinner next week," the Marquis promised, "and I swear that you will not be disappointed."

"I have never been disappointed by anything in your house," Harriette answered. "Your food, like the decor, is outstanding."

She smiled and went on:

"It is interesting how every man has some attribute concerning which he spreads his tail like a peacock. Yours is a superlative cuisine."

"I am not arguing about that," the Marquis remarked.

"Lord Yarmouth's is antiques. When I last dined with him he showed me a collection of gold and silver coins, portraits, snuff boxes and watches of which he was justifiably proud."

The Marquis looked bored.

"Lord Yarmouth has also a love-nest in Hyde Park," Harriette said.

The Marquis appeared more interested.

"It consists of a small sitting-room and a bed-chamber," Harriette explained. "He opens the door himself and it is very discreet."

She laughed.

"He told me how he discovered by chance that a very important lady was having an intrigue with a young Dragoon. He only proposed to keep her secret on condition she made him as happy as she had made the Dragoon.

" 'Was that honourable?' I asked him.

" 'Perhaps not,' he replied, 'but I couldn't help it!' "

The Marquis laughed.

"The Regent's pride and joy, like yours, is his food," Harriette went on. "I can't imagine why you wish to upset him. You know as well as I do that he loathes being beaten at his own game. He has been extolling Carême's virtues ever since he brought him over from France."

"I have heard that theme on innumerable occasions," the Marquis said.

"And so you intend to make His Royal Highness take second place," Harriette said. "Well quite frankly, I think it unkind of you."

Then she laughed.

"All the same it is typical! Do you always get what you want? That of course being the victor's crown?"

"Always!" the Marquis replied.

She made a grimace at him.

"You are insufferably conceited!" she teased. "At the same time you have plenty of justification for it."

The Marquis raised her hand to his lips.

"Thank you, Harriette."

She knew it was not only for the compliment.

He moved towards the door and to her own annoyance she was forced to ask the question she thought should have come from him.

"When shall I see you again?"

"I will be in touch with you," he answered, "and you shall definitely enjoy Bouvais's food within the next few days."

He shut the door of Harriette's room behind him and she stood hearing his footsteps going down the stairs before she flung herself down on the crumpled silk sheets of her bed.

She had the feeling that the Marquis had defeated her

again, and it was a sensation that she had never experienced with any other man.

The Marquis, however, drove back to Wayne House tooling his High-Perch Phaeton despite the fact that it was still raining.

If there was one thing he disliked it was being shut up in a closed carriage. It gave him the feeling of being confined, and that was something he could never endure.

The rain on his face, the wind that had a touch of chill in it, seemed to him positively invigorating, and as he stepped down from the Phaeton outside his porticoed front door he looked the picture of vigorous, athletic good health.

As soon as the Butler had taken his high-crowned hat and a footman his many-tiered overcoat, the Marquis walked across the marble hall towards the library.

"Tell Major Brownlow that I wish to speak to him," he said to the footman who opened the door.

"Very good, M'Lord."

On the Marquis's desk was, as he expected, a list of those who had accepted his invitation to dine that evening.

He was not surprised, as anyone else might have been, to find that although the invitations had gone out only that morning, there had been no refusals.

The Regent was bringing with him two distinguished foreign visitors who were staying with him at Carlton House, and in addition the party would include the Marquis's most intimate friends.

Amongst them was Lord Alvanley who had dined with him the night before, and the General.

The Marquis had hesitated over the General's name. Then he thought it would be bad manners not to include him when it was his Chef who was providing the main entertainment of the evening.

He was also extremely curious as to where the General could have found Bouvais.

He was well aware of the straitened circumstances in which his previous Commanding Officer lived, and although he had tried last night to discover where Bouvais had worked in the past, he had been unsuccessful in learning anything about the man.

He thought he would prime the Prince Regent to ask a few questions which the General might have difficulty in refusing to answer; if the Prince failed, there was always Lord Yarmouth.

Lord Yarmouth, son of the Marquis of Hertford, was a close friend of His Royal Highness, despite the fact that his mother was believed to be the Regent's mistress.

There were those who said that in the circumstances Yarmouth, if he was a gentleman, should refuse to associate with the heir to the throne.

Lord Yarmouth had his enemies, and had been black-balled from becoming a member of White's.

This however did not spoil his social career because he had great charm, generosity and a real knowledge, as Harriette had found, of everything that was best in art.

This was irresistible to the Regent, and they spent a great deal of time together buying pictures and forming a collection of works of art which the Marquis was certain would one day in the far future be a national asset.

He was staring at the list of guests he held in his hand when the door opened and Major Brownlow came in.

He had recently dispensed with the crutch which he had used after he was wounded, and now had a wooden leg and walked with a stick.

He had however to move slowly and as his secretary walked towards him, the Marquis indicated a chair on the other side of the desk.

"I am hoping, Brownlow," he said, "that tonight's dinner will be as good as the one we enjoyed last night."

"I hope so too, My Lord."

"You have told the Chef that His Royal Highness will be present?"

There was a moment's hesitation before Major Brownlow replied:

"He has been informed, My Lord."

"And you have seen a copy of the menu?"

"I have it here," Major Brownlow answered. "Henson

gave it to me about half-an-hour ago, when the Chef arrived."

The Marquis looked puzzled.

"When the Chef arrived?" he repeated. "Do you mean he was not here early to-day?"

"I understand that Bouvais brings a great many of the dishes already prepared, My Lord," Major Brownlow answered. "He prefers to work that way, and as he is only temporarily employed I saw no reason to question any arrangements he wished to make."

"Quite so," the Marquis agreed. "But it seems strange. And I presume he buys the food and makes a profit out of it?"

"I doubt it," Major Brownlow answered. "He sent the bills to me yesterday and I have received some to-day. Everything had been bought in the best markets. Although he paid in cash, it would be difficult for him to make any additions to the invoices."

The Marquis raised his eye-brows.

"Then if he is not making a bit on the side, he is certainly different from any of the Chefs we have employed in the past."

"He is indeed, My Lord."

"You know, Brownlow," the Marquis said, sitting down at his desk, "I think that, expensive though this man is, we should employ him permanently."

"I have already thought of that, My Lord, and it would certainly be wise to take him on until the end of the season when I presume you will be leaving for the country, unless you go to Brighton with His Royal Highness."

"I think it would be a mistake not to keep him," the Marquis replied. "He may not wish to leave London; if so, when I am away, he can stay here doing nothing. It would be better than losing him altogether."

"Exactly what I was thinking myself, My Lord," Major Brownlow said.

"What sort of man is he?" the Marquis asked.

Again Major Brownlow hesitated, then as he realised the Marquis was waiting for an answer, he said:

"To tell you the truth, My Lord, I have not actually seen him!"

"Not seen him?" the Marquis ejaculated. "Why not?"

"I suggested that he should come to my office before dinner last night after I had sent him his fee for the evening, and also paid the bills for the food. But Bouvais replied through Henson that he could not leave the kitchen at that particular moment."

"That is of course understandable," the Marquis conceded,

"When you sent the message after the first course to say that you were giving another dinner tonight," Major Brownlow went on, "I told Henson that I would like Bouvais to speak to me before he left the house. Unfortunately he could not have understood my request, for when I enquired the man had already left."

"Perhaps he has a nervous temperament," the Marquis suggested. "Well, for God's sake, do not upset him, Brownlow, before dinner. You know what these Frenchmen are like!"

"I do indeed, My Lord," Major Brownlow agreed.

"If he wants to be retiring, let him be," the Marquis ordered. "In the meantime, tell him I expect him to stay on indefinitely, provided that his food is as satisfactory as it is at the moment."

"I am sure he will be very gratified, My Lord, but it is a phenomenal figure to pay. Perhaps he will accept less if it is on a permanent basis."

"It is really of no consequence," the Marquis said in a bored voice. "If one wants the best, as you and I have found so often, one has to pay for it!"

"That is true, My Lord."

. . . . . .

Downstairs in the kitchen, Araminta's dishes were receiving exclamations of admiration from the servants crowded round the kitchen-table.

Last night they had been entranced by the sugar-basket which Caro had made, but this evening they were even more thrilled by a large white swan which carried on its back crystalized red cherries.

Swimming on a pool of green jelly, surrounded by golden kingcups with leaves of angelica, the soteltie was a picture of real beauty.

Caro had also had time to make a little witch's house in barley sugar encompassed by spotted mushrooms.

It was a child's dish, but Araminta had learnt that the hedgehog had been a great success and she thought that the gentlemen would be just as delighted with a fairy-tale cottage.

The dishes she had chosen were again some of her father's favourites, especially *Rognons Sautés au Champagne,* kidneys cooked in champagne and *Timbale de filets de Sole Cardinal* which was soles folded over sliced lobster with small mushrooms, then encircled with slices of truffle.

Araminta had been rather worried in case the soles were not fresh, but Hannah had declared that she was satisfied and hers was a judgement which could not be questioned.

Araminta regretted that it was not the right time of year for partridge, pheasant, woodcock or snipe, all of which she could cook in a manner that she was quite certain the Marquis had never previously enjoyed.

But there were ortolans and quails which were delicious – *à la Richelieu* or with *Château Yquem* and sauces from all parts of Europe with which she could disguise the more familiar ducks, geese and chicken.

As her father would have appreciated, the Marquis's wines had made a great difference.

The Butler had been considerably startled when Araminta had demanded not only vintage champagne for the cooking, but also the Marquis's best claret, his finest brandy, and a port which he intended only to be drunk with reverence.

"Gustave only used the cheaper wines, Miss Bouvais," he said reproachfully.

"I am not Gustave!" Araminta retorted, "and my dishes require the very best wines obtainable."

Grumbling a little beneath his breath, Mr. Henson had obliged by bringing the bottles Araminta required and putting them down on the table almost defiantly.

"It seems to me to be a great waste," he said. "Wines should be drunk alone, not mixed up with a lot of flummery!"

"When you taste the sauces I shall make with them you will understand why they are important," Araminta smiled.

She was well aware that the Butler, of whom all the other servants stood in considerable awe, had already capitulated completely where she was concerned.

He had in fact been proud, she knew, to carry her dishes into the dining-room and see how greatly they were appreciated by the Gentlemen seated around the Marquis's table.

He had described to Araminta how, when the sugar-basket had been set in front of the Marquis, he had raised his glass to the General and said:

"I withdraw, General! You are undoubtedly the winner of this contest, as no-body here will deny!"

"I am glad you are satisfied," the General replied gravely.

He could not prevent the smile on his lips or his eyes from twinkling.

"What are you going to say to the Regent?" Lord Alvanley enquired. "You will have to tell him because everyone in White's is waiting for the result of tonight's meal."

The Marquis laughed.

"I shall merely say: *'Le Roi est mort! Vive le Roi!'*"

"He will never rest until he takes this man away from you," Lord Alvanley chuckled.

"I have a feeling that it will be over my dead body!" the Marquis answered.

They had all laughed at this and the Butler hurried below stairs to tell Araminta what had been said.

Henson could only stay for a moment and as he turned away he said over his shoulder:

"Don't forget, Miss Bouvais, that Major Brownlow wishes to see you afore you leave."

Araminta had waited until he was gone, then she said to Jim the boot-boy who had originally let her into the house.

"Would you be very kind and call me a hackney carriage?"

"Yes, of course, Miss," he answered.

The boys were already her slaves because she had fed them tit-bits of the puddings while she was decorating the dishes.

"*Monsieur* Gustave never let us touch anything in the kitchen," one of them said.

"I would not like you to touch anything I had made," Araminta answered, "but what I give you is a very different thing. There is quite a lot of chocolate mousse left in the bowl, which I suggest you divide amongst you."

She did not have to speak twice and the chocolate mousse disappeared in a few large mouthfuls.

She thought that if she came again to Wayne House, she and Hannah would make a little extra of the puddings so that there would be enough left over for the boys.

She had slipped out of the house as soon as Jim had found a hackney carriage for her, and by the time the Butler came downstairs to remind her that Major Brownlow was waiting to see her, she had left.

She had, however, already learnt that she was to return the following day and all the way home she was planning her menu and making a mental list of everything she would require.

She told Hannah of her success, wrote down what they must buy in the markets and jumped into bed.

'I must hurry and get to sleep,' she thought, 'or I will never be able to wake up at five o'clock.'

She had reckoned however without Hannah who, instead of waking her as she had done the previous morning, let her sleep.

When Araminta finally opened her eyes the old maid was pulling back the curtains and had brought her breakfast upstairs to her.

"What is the time?" she asked.

"Nearly nine o'clock, Miss Araminta."

Araminta sat up in bed and gave a little shriek.

"Oh, Hannah, how could you have let me sleep so late? You know we have to go to the markets this morning."

"I've been to them already," Hannah answered.

"Hannah, you should not have done that!"

"You wants your sleep – tiring yourself out standing on stone floors half the night! I know what it's like!"

"It's not as tiring as getting up at five o'clock to haggle with all those market-men," Araminta retorted.

"Now don't you go worrying your head about that," Hannah replied. "Everything's downstairs and I haven't forgotten a thing!"

"I am sure you have not," Araminta said, "and it was sweet of you, Hannah, really it was. But it is not right that I should give you all this extra work."

"I'm doing it for the same reason you are, Miss Araminta, – for Master Harry. So let's hope he's grateful – the young varmint!"

Hannah went from the room shutting the door sharply behind her and Araminta had to laugh.

It was so like Hannah to scold Harry and be extremely angry with him, and at the same time to be prepared to kill herself if necessary in an effort to help him.

"After all, tonight, we will have £40!" Araminta said to herself, thinking with satisfaction of the envelope lying on her dressing-table, which the Butler had handed to her the previous evening.

Once again she thought how wonderful it would be if she could make enough in time without having to ask her mother to sell her engagement ring.

She knew it would hurt Lady Sinclair more than anything else to part with the ring she had worn all her married life.

"I must make enough to save Mama from having to give it up."

Araminta was well aware that today it was going to be very difficult to keep Lady Sinclair from knowing what was going on.

For one thing she would wish to take her daughter to the shops.

For another, Araminta had to find an explanation as to why she would be leaving the house early in the afternoon and not returning until after midnight.

It was Caro who, coming into Araminta's room a few minutes later, provided a solution.

"You know that Harry is trying to sell his horses this afternoon?" she asked, sitting down on Araminta's bed.

"Yes, I know," Araminta answered. "I hope he gets a good price for them."

"What I suggest," Caro said, "is that you could say that you are going with him to meet some of his friends. I will keep Mama engaged in the small sitting-room at the back of the house while you and Hannah are loading up the hackney carriage."

She paused before she finished:

"There is another thing, Araminta: I think it would be dangerous to take Hannah with you. Mama is sure to ask where she has gone."

"I can quite well manage on my own," Araminta answered, "and the moment I arrive the kitchen-boys will be only too willing to help me. Hannah and I will make them a whole dish of trifle for themselves."

"Then that is settled," Caro said, "and as Mama is still feeling rather tired this morning, I can easily dissuade her from wishing to go shopping."

"What are we going to say if I have to go out again to-morrow?" Araminta enquired.

"I refuse to cross any bridges until we come to them," Caro answered. "All this plotting and planning is very hard on the mind!"

Araminta laughed.

"I think the truth is, Caro, that living in the country, we have not used our minds enough. It will do us good to intrigue a little and sharpen up our wits."

"With which to puzzle the *Beau Monde*?" Caro asked ironically.

Araminta gave a little sigh.

"It is no use thinking of what we might have done," she answered. "As soon as Harry is safe we must go back to the country. We will not be able to afford to stay here. Besides .. what would be the point?"

"We have to tell Mama."

"Of course we will have to tell her," Araminta agreed,

"but quite frankly, Caro, I think it is only fair that Harry should do it."

"He will not like that," Caro answered.

"It is right that he should put himself out a little," Araminta insisted.

Then, as usual, her soft heart defeated her.

"I know . . I will tell Mama," she said. "I can make Harry sound more pathetic than he can make himself, and as Mama loves him you know she will not be angry for long."

"I do not mind her being angry," Caro answered. 'It is when she is sad and broken-hearted that it is unbearable."

Araminta thought the same but she told herself she had to be practical. The only thing that must concern her at the moment was to clear Harry of his debt to the Marquis.

She dressed quickly and went downstairs to the kitchen.

She worked all the morning. By luncheon-time she could relax a little and talk lightly and inconsequentially with her mother without worrying too much about the evening which lay ahead.

Only occasionally did her mind go back to that horrifying moment when she had found the cat dead on the larder floor and realised that the *crème brûlée* had been poisoned.

Although she tried not to think of it she was in fact rather apprehensive that one of the other dishes might after all have been tampered with.

It was a relief when on reaching Wayne House she found two of the pantry-boys waiting for her and saw by the smiles of welcome on their faces that they had no bad news to impart.

Nevertheless, when everything had been brought down to the kitchen, Araminta could not help asking if the Marquis was in good health.

"I hope His Lordship has not suffered any ill-effects from my dinner?" she enquired.

"That he hasn't," one of the servants answered. "In fact Mr. Jenkins – His Lordship's valet – was saying as he'd never seen His Lordship in such good spirits as he was this morning. Pleased as Punch with the dinner, Mr. Jenkins says!"

72

"And 'em as had put their money on you, Miss Bouvais, 'll be pleased all right," a footman said.

"I wonder if the bets were very large ones," Araminta remarked.

"Mr. Jenkins says as how th'gentlemen at White's Club are always ready to wager a fortune! An' not only on the turn of a card! Indeed, they bets on th'daftest things."

"What sort of things?" Araminta asked.

She was decorating one of the dishes, as she spoke, with the curling leaves of small lettuces and cutting tomatoes and radishes into the shape of flowers.

She had already set two of the kitchen-maids to slicing oranges and lemons to give the other dishes colour.

"One gentlemen," the footman went on, "bet three thousand pounds one wet day on which two drops of rain would slide down first to the bottom of a window-pane."

"How ridiculous!" Araminta exclaimed.

"His Lordship 'ad a bet as to th' date Napoleon Bonaparte'd enter Paris," another footman interposed.

"Did he win?" Araminta asked.

" 'e always wins!," the footman replied, "on a mill, on th' race-course, an' on th' cards!"

Araminta's lips tightened.

She had already formed a dislike for the Marquis of Wayne and she thought now that it was insufferable that any man should be so successful and obviously so pleased about it.

At the same time she could not ignore the note of pride in the footman's voice.

'They think he is wonderful!' she thought scornfully.

But she was too wise to say anything and merely continued to decorate the dishes and make everything look so attractive that the kitchen and scullery maids were in ecstasies.

It was now time to start cooking, but this evening when the staff went to the servants hall for their meal Araminta did not go with them.

She was taking no chances on Gustave or anyone else coming back to add poison to her food.

She had an idea that he would not attempt the same method a second time, but she was not prepared to take the risk.

She wondered if the Chef had hung around the house early that morning waiting to hear if the Marquis was still alive or if in fact his plan had mis-fired and one of His Lordship's guests was dead.

It was an uneasy feeling to think that he might be watching, waiting and hoping for revenge.

Then she told herself that it was none of her business.

All she must be careful of was to see that no crime was committed in which she could be implicated, and nothing could occur while she was at Wayne House which could reflect adversely upon Harry.

She therefore worked on in the kitchen and sooner than she expected, because they felt ashamed of letting her do all the work, the kitchen-maids returned to help her.

Mr. Henson, the Butler, came into the kitchen after the servants' meal was finished to look at the dishes arranged on the side-tables and to express his approval.

"You have a hard task in front of you tonight, Miss Bouvais," he said. "I hear from the Butler at Carlton House that His Royal Highness is so delighted with Antoine Carême that he would like to give him a medal."

Araminta laughed.

"How awkward if I should ask for one too!"

"Well, from all I see, you deserve it, Miss Bouvais. To tell you the truth, I've never had such fine food, looking so pretty, to carry into any dining-room!"

"Mr. Henson, you overwhelm me!"

"I means it, Miss Bouvais! the Butler insisted, "and if he was to see you, I don't think His Lordship would believe it possible!"

"He still thinks I am a man?" Araminta asked quickly.

"He does, Miss Bouvais! And so does Major Brownlow. He grumbled about your leaving before he had a chance of seeing you last night, but I told him you were very temperamental-like, and shy when it comes to meeting strangers."

"That was kind of you, Mr. Henson."

Araminta produced the bills for the purchases Hannah had made that morning in the markets.

"I wonder if you would be kind enough to take these to Major Brownlow?" she asked. "You will understand that I will want to slip away as soon as dinner is finished."

"I expect he has your money ready, Miss Bouvais," the Butler said, "but anyway I'll go and find out."

"That is very kind of you," Araminta said.

The Butler left the kitchen and when he returned a quarter-of-an-hour later he carried an envelope in his hand which he put down beside Araminta.

"There's your fee, Miss Bouvais," he said, "and Major Brownlow asks if you'd step upstairs when you have finished dishing up the dinner to collect the money that he owes you for the food."

Araminta was still.

"He will not give it to you, Mr. Henson?" she asked.

The Butler shook his head.

"I tried to persuade him, Miss Bouvais, I did really, but he wishes to speak to you, he says."

"What do you think it is about?" Araminta asked apprehensively.

"Well, if you ask me, Miss Bouvais, I think he's going to offer you the position here permanent."

Araminta looked at him wide-eyed.

"Permanent?" she repeated faintly.

"Yes, Miss Bouvais."

She had hoped to get enough engagements in the next week to pay off Harry's debt, but she had not contemplated that the Marquis might wish to employ her on a permanent basis.

The Butler saw her hesitation and after a moment said:

"We'd be glad to have you, Miss Bouvais, and I think we could all work well together."

"Thank you, Mr. Henson," Araminta smiled at him, "but I am afraid that is impossible. Do you think you could tell Major Brownlow that while I am delighted to come for the next few days, perhaps until the end of the next week, I could not make any further promises?"

"Do you mean that?" the Butler enquired, "or is it that you've got the chance of a better situation?"

"No, no, of course not!" Araminta said. "It is just that I . . ."

She thought wildly what she would say, then added:

". . I may be going abroad, perhaps back to France."

"I'm sorry about that, Miss Bouvais."

"You are very kind, Mr. Henson, but if I was always here you might easily grow tired of me."

The Butler waited a moment, then he said:

"Do you wish me to tell Major Brownlow what you have just told me?"

"We can leave it until he asks," Araminta replied, "but please see if you can persuade him to repay me the money that I spent this morning. I shall want it if I am to buy more food for tomorrow."

As she spoke she wondered how long she and Hannah would be able to continue getting up so early in the morning to visit the markets.

'Tomorrow,' Araminta decided, 'I must go alone, or perhaps Caro will come with me. I cannot expect Hannah to do so much.'

At the same time she knew that if she rose at five and stayed late at Wayne House she would be very tired if she had to do it for a week.

'This really is a man's job,' she told herself and wondered a little whimsically how they would fare if Harry had to do the shopping for a change.

The Butler came back a little later in triumph

"Major Brownlow has given me the money, Miss Bouvais," he said, "but he insists that tomorrow afternoon you go up to see him as soon as you arrive."

"Is there a dinner-party tomorrow night?" Araminta asked.

"The Major didn't say," the Butler replied. "I'll try and find out before you leave."

"I must know if I am to go to the markets early in the morning," Araminta answered.

"*Monsieur* Gustave used to have things delivered," the

Butler suggested. "He would give an order at the beginning
of the week, for so much fish, so much meat and the other
things he required, and if we didn't finish them all they were
just thrown away."

"That is quite an unnecessary extravagance," Araminta
said. "Besides, in that way one does not always get fresh
food."

"That's true," the Butler agreed, "but not all Chefs are as
conscientious as you, Miss Bouvais. They doll things up with
a bit of sauce and, if it tastes all right, it doesn't matter
what's underneath!"

"In which case you might as well be eating sawdust!"
Araminta snapped. "I call it dishonest, and that is exactly
what it is!"

"As I've already said, Miss Bouvais, you're different
from any of the Chefs I've ever worked with, and that's a
compliment!"

"Thank you," Araminta smiled.

The Butler glanced at the clock, gave an exclamation and
hurried away upstairs.

The dinner was an unqualified success – there was no
doubt about that!

The footmen coming down to fetch the dishes related
gleefully the Regent's astonishment at the appearance of
each new dish and the compliments they heard being expressed all round the table.

"It seems the gentry can talk of nothing else but food!"
one of them said.

Another remarked:

"They're all a-eating as if they've never seen food a-fore –
like porkers round a trough, they be!"

Araminta laughed.

At the same time, when dinner was finished she felt very
tired.

It was hot in the kitchen, her cheeks were burning and
there were little tendrils of curls around her forehead from
the heat and steam of the stove.

Finally when the oven was empty and the table was bare
she picked up her cloak and said to Jim:

"Will you find me a hackney carriage?"

"Yes, of course, Miss."

He sped away and Araminta sat down for a moment on one of the hard wooden chairs.

Hannah was right, she thought: it was tiring on the feet to stand for long on stone flags.

Jim re-appeared and she looked at him in surprise. He had only been gone a few seconds.

"There were a carriage just outside," he said, "so I didn't have to go far."

"Thank you, Jim."

Araminta pulled her hood over her fair hair and ran up the basement steps.

Drawn up outside was a hackney carriage pulled by one of the thin, tired old horses that were usually to be found on the streets at night.

She glanced up at the driver.

"Number 3 Russell Square, please."

Jim opened the door and she got in quickly because it was still raining.

As the door shut the carriage started off and Araminta leant back.

Then she gave a scream of sheer terror as she suddenly realised that she was not alone in the carriage.

There was a man sitting beside her in the darkness!

CHAPTER FOUR

"It is all right," a voice said. "Do not be frightened."

"But .. I am .. frightened," Araminta exclaimed. "Why are you .. here in my .. carriage?"

"I was waiting for you," the man replied.

"Waiting for .. me?"

The terror she had felt when she first knew someone was in the carriage with her was now less intense.

But she was still trembling, and what made it so uncanny was that it was impossible to see the man's face in the darkness.

However he sounded quite a young man, and after a moment Araminta managed to control her voice a little better although her heart was still thumping wildly.

"Why do you .. wish to .. see me?" she asked.

"I want you to help me."

"To help .. you?" she repeated in surprise. "Then why did you have to .. wait outside the .. house and .. surprise me in such an .. unpleasant manner?"

"I did not know your name. In fact, I was expecting you to be a man."

"Then how .." Araminta began, only to be interrupted as the man beside her continued:

"Last night I heard the boy tell the hackney carriage he had fetched to wait for the Chef. When you stepped into it I could not believe that you were the cook!"

"Why were you .. waiting?" Araminta asked.

She was almost certain that she already knew the answer to that question before he replied:

"I had a reason – and a very good one!"

Araminta drew in her breath.

"Are you .. Gustave?"

"No," the man beside her replied. "But I think you have a good idea why I was waiting to see if Gustave had been successful."

"You .. knew that he had .. put poison in one of the dishes?" Araminta asked hesitatingly.

"I gave him the poison!"

"But ..why? Why?" Araminta asked. "Why should you .. wish to .. kill the Marquis? In a way I can .. understand Gustave being furious because he had been .. dismissed, but .. how are .. you involved?"

There was a pause before the man said slowly and distinctly:

"Because if the Marquis does not die – I must kill myself!"

Araminta was still.

The carriage was proceeding slowly through the streets. Suddenly in the light of a linkman's flare she had a quick glimpse of the man beside her.

She had been right. He was young. He seemed also, from what she could see of him and the way he spoke, to be a gentleman.

"Perhaps," she said in a voice she hoped sounded calm and unhysterical, "you will .. explain exactly what you are .. trying to do."

"I am trying to kill the Marquis, and I hope he rots in hell, damn him!"

"What has he .. done to you?"

There was a silence that was somehow ominous.

Then her companion said:

"I owe him £20,000!"

Araminta gave a little cry which she could not prevent.

"£20,000!" she exclaimed. "But how? Can you .. have lost so much at .. cards?"

"Is there any other way in this blasted world of losing so much money?" the man asked savagely.

"But if you .. kill the Marquis .." Araminta began.

"He has to be dead by the end of next week. I imagine you were responsible for seeing he did not die last night. How did you prevent the dish which Gustave poisoned from reaching the dining-table?"

"It killed the .. cat!"

The man beside her gave an exclamation half of anger and half of hopelessness.

"Even fate is against me! If I had any sense, I would blow a piece of lead through my brain and have done with it!"

"No, no! You must not do .. that!" Araminta cried. "There must be .. some other .. way."

"The only other way is for me to kill the Marquis, and anyway he deserves to die."

"Why should you say .. that?"

"Because he constitutes a challenge to fools like me, because he is so devilishly lucky, because he is always the winner! It is only human nature to try to put an end to his run of luck."

Araminta did not speak.

It seemed to her that this young man was saying just the same as Harry had.

"I intend to kill him," the man went on, "and I shall save not only my family from destruction, but also innumerable other young fools from falling into the same trap."

"It was to save your family?" Araminta questioned.

The man beside her drew a deep breath and she knew it was one of pain.

"How could you have been so foolish as to gamble so highly when you knew you could not afford to lose?" Araminta asked.

She spoke passionately because it seemed to her at this moment that she was speaking not to a stranger, but as it were to her brother.

"You do not understand what it is like to sit at the gaming-table and watch the turn of a card," the man beside her said in a low voice. "One becomes mesmerised and loses all sense of values. Money means nothing! It is the excitement of winning that counts, or the anticipation that one might."

He was silent and the horse drawing the carriage plodded on. Once again in a passing light Araminta had a glimpse of her companion's profile.

He was, she thought again, extremely young, and she

imagined that like Harry he would want to behave like a man of fashion, to do what young men did without their financial backing to support him.

"There must be some way of .. finding the money," she said, "without having to resort to .. murder."

"I was going to ask you to kill the Marquis for me."

Araminta made a sharp movement of revulsion and he said quickly:

"But I thought you were a man, and I know now you would never consent to do such a thing."

"No, of course not!" Araminta replied. "But how could you imagine that any decent man, let alone woman, would stoop to such a crime?"

"Most people in your position will do anything for money," her companion said cynically. "Gustave was only too pleased to accept the £100 I gave him!"

"Do you realise that, if your plan had succeeded, it is I who would have been suspected of the crime and not Gustave?" Araminta asked.

"He thought of that," the man beside her answered. "In fact he said he hoped that the new Chef would hang for it!"

"How appalling!" Araminta murmured almost beneath her breath.

"He did not imagine that the Chef might be a woman like you."

"That does not make it any less shocking," she said severely. "You had no right to tempt a servant, especially a foreigner, to commit a crime on your behalf which .."

She stopped.

"Which I was too cowardly to do myself," her companion finished. "That is what you are thinking, is it not?"

"I believe .. murder, whatever the provocation, to be a crime against all decency," Araminta replied.

"The Marquis has to die!"

"And if he does and you are suspected of his death you will .. hang."

"I shall not be suspected!" he muttered.

"No, I will!" Araminta snapped. "And quite frankly .. I have no intention of dying on your .. behalf!"

"Then I will shoot him; and if I am unable to do that, I will shoot myself!"

As he spoke he drew something from his pocket and Araminta was certain that it was a pistol.

"Please .. you are frightening .. me again," she said in a trembling voice.

"I have no wish to frighten you. Will you accept £200—£500 if you like – to put poison in one of the dishes which the Marquis will eat tomorrow?"

Araminta did not answer and he went on:

"You owe me that much, considering that it was you who circumvented Gustave's efforts."

"You are being ridiculous!" Araminta answered, "and you well know it. Of course I have no intention of murdering the Marquis. If I were convicted of the crime and not hanged for it, I would certainly be transported."

"No, that must not happen," the man beside her conceded. "In which case I had best shoot myself immediately. Then there will be no more problems."

He spoke in such a wild manner that Araminta was seriously frightened.

She had the feeling that he might put his threat into action immediately.

Apart from the horror of it, she would have to explain to the Magistrates why she was driving in a hackney carriage late at night with a man she did not know and who had not even told her his name.

"Please .. put your pistol away," she pleaded, "and let us discuss this .. sensibly. Perhaps I can .. help."

"Could you really?"

She felt he was clutching at a straw, and she wondered wildly how it would be possible to help him, to prevent him from killing himself.

"Give me the .. pistol," she said, putting out her hand.

She thought he would refuse. Then he put something very cold and heavy into her hand and she laid it on the seat on the other side of her, hoping it would not go off by mistake.

"Let us start at the .. beginning," she said. "Will you tell me your name?"

"It is Yeoman," he answered. "Lord Yeoman, although a lot of good my title will do me now."

"Mine is Araminta .. Bouvais."

"I am sure you are very pretty," he said, "in fact the glimpse I had of you last night told me you were a very unusual sort of cook."

"We are talking about you," Araminta said gently. "Is there no other way you can find £20,000 except by selling your home?"

"None that I know of," Lord Yeoman answered. "My father is seventy and in ill-health. My mother is younger but very frail, and I think when they learn what a fool their son has made of himself it will kill them both!"

"I can understand your .. feeling like .. that," Araminta said, thinking of her mother.

Lord Yeoman put his hands up to his eyes.

"I cannot go home and tell my father what a fool I have made of myself."

"I am sure he would be more .. understanding than you expect."

"He will know it is a debt of honour and that it must be paid," Lord Yeoman replied.

Araminta was silent, and they drove on for a little while before he said:

"If only Gustave's effort had succeeded or you were a different sort of person! The Marquis would die quickly without much pain, and I would be saved!"

'So would Harry,' Araminta thought to herself, then felt ashamed.

"The only alternative to killing the Marquis is for me to die," Lord Yeoman said despairingly. "If I were dead, I imagine he would not press my parents to honour the debt, and perhaps it would be possible for me to make it look like an accident."

"It is morbid and quite ridiculous to talk in such a manner," Araminta replied. "Can you imagine anything more nonsensical than for a young man to kill himself for a gambling debt? You have all your life in front of you, with so many fine and better things you can do instead of dying like a coward."

"I said you would think of me as a coward," Lord Yeoman said defiantly.

"Suicide is a coward's way out."

"If I had only myself to think of, I would pay the Marquis and then sit outside his house in rags begging for scraps and hoping he would be ashamed of the condition to which he had brought me."

He gave a short laugh which had no humour in it.

"Instead I shall be obliged to haunt him. Do you think he will be afraid of clanking chains or of phantoms with their heads under their arms?"

Araminta did not speak and Lord Yeoman cried loudly:

"I hate and detest him! I loathe and abhor him! Curse him! Curse him for what he has done to me and a lot of other men like me!"

The violence with which he spoke seemed to vibrate around the confines of the carriage and ring in Araminta's ears.

She knew they were nearing Russell Square and that she must think of some way to help this young man before she left him.

She was certain that in the miserable state he was in he was quite capable of taking his own life as he had threatened to do.

If he did, she thought, it would always be on her conscience that she had not somehow saved him.

Then she realised that beside her Lord Yeoman was weeping.

Instinctively she put out her hand and laid it on his arm.

"I am sorry," she said gently. "So very . . sorry."

He did not answer her, but there was no doubt that he was crying tempestuously into his hands.

'I must help him . . I must!' she thought to herself.

At that moment the carriage came to a stop outside her house.

Araminta made up her mind.

"I tell you what I will do," she said. "I will talk to the Marquis. I will try to persuade him to forget your debt because of the effect it would have on your father and mother."

"He will never do that," Lord Yeoman said hoarsely. "A gaming debt has always to be paid."

"Not if the creditor decides he has no wish for the money," Araminta said firmly.

"It would be dishonourable of me."

"It would be far more dishonourable of you to .. kill him."

"He will not listen to you."

"I will try to .. make him."

"I should not let you do so."

Lord Yeoman did not speak very positively and Araminta fancied there was a note of hope in his voice.

"Leave it to me," she said firmly. "If I fail .. then we will have to think of .. something else. But you must promise me that you will do nothing drastic until I have seen the Marquis."

"Do you really intend to speak to him?" Lord Yeoman asked.

"I will talk to him," Araminta promised. "Where can I get in touch with you?"

"At White's Club," Lord Yeoman answered, "or perhaps I could meet you at your home?"

"No, you must not come here," Araminta said quickly. "I will send a note to you at White's telling you either what the Marquis has decided or where we can meet."

"It is very kind of you to do this."

"I think rather it is very brave," Araminta corrected. "I have never met the Marquis, but I have a feeling he is very awe-inspiring."

"He is!"

There was something young in the way Lord Yeoman spoke and Araminta asked:

"May I enquire how old you are?"

"I am twenty-one and two months, so I have not the excuse of being a minor."

"Perhaps that is a pity."

86

"I am a man," Lord Yeoman said, "and I should stand up to my own responsibilities. But, as you see, I am not only a fool, I am also a helpless one!"

"You have only done what a great many other young men do when they first come to London. As you said yourself, the gaming-tables are mesmeric."

She realised that she must leave him and said quietly:

"I have your promise to do nothing .. foolish until you hear from me?"

"I have given you my word."

"And will you also forget where you have brought me in this hackney carriage? I have reasons for not wishing anyone at Wayne House to know my address."

"You can trust me not to tell anyone where we now are," Lord Yeoman said.

"Then I think I had better go in," Araminta replied. "Will you allow me to .. pay the cabman?"

"I would consider that an insult if I did not realise that you meant it kindly."

"Then thank you for bringing me home," Araminta said, "and because I believe I can trust you .. and also because it .. frightens me .. I will leave that unpleasant .. weapon on the seat beside you."

"I have told you that you may trust me," Lord Yeoman answered.

He opened the door, stepped out and helped Araminta to alight.

Hannah had put a lantern over the doorway to enable her to find her way up the steps.

In the light of it Araminta and Lord Yeoman looked at each other.

She saw that he was quite good-looking although rather thin, and she was sure that he was unusually sensitive for a man of his age.

"As I thought, you are very pretty," he said, "and I am more grateful to you than I can ever express in words."

He raised her hand to his lips, kissed it and waited while Araminta went up the steps and opened the door with the key which Hannah had given her.

She turned to wave to him, then shut the door firmly.

Inside the house she suddenly felt extremely weak and exhausted.

She had been tired before she left Wayne House, but the drama which Lord Yeoman had forced on her seemed to have sapped her strength to the point where it was hard to walk up the stairs.

Finally, clinging to the banisters, she dragged herself up the two flights which led to the bed-rooms.

It was very quiet and Araminta knew that the household was asleep.

She had a sudden longing to go to her mother, as she would have done when she was a child, to find help and a solution for the problem which confronted her.

Then she told herself that no-one must know what had occurred tonight.

She had a feeling that Caro, who was more practical than she was, would think it ridiculous of her to concern herself with Lord Yeoman's troubles when they had enough of their own.

And how could she plead for his debt to be cancelled when they were all so deeply involved in finding the £600 which Harry owed to the Marquis?

But it seemed to Araminta now as it had seemed at the time, that she could not possibly refuse to help the unhappy young man.

If he killed himself, she knew she would feel responsible.

At the same time, the thought of approaching the Marquis was very frightening and as she got into bed Araminta found she was trembling.

* * * * * *

If she had been frightened the night before, she was even more frightened the following day when she set off for Wayne House immediately after luncheon.

She had no idea whether there was to be a party or not, but she imagined that if there was to be one of any importance the Marquis or Major Brownlow would have sent her a message through the General.

As it was she was grateful for an excuse not to rise early and drag Hannah to the Markets.

She knew there was enough food in the larder at Wayne House to supply a meal for a dozen people.

If after she had talked with Major Brownlow, anything unusual was required, she would be able to buy it at the shops in Shepherds Market which catered for the aristocratic houses in the neighbourhood.

She was having coffee with her mother and Caro at eleven o'clock when the General was announced by Hannah.

Lady Sinclair looked up with pleasure.

She always welcomed a visit from the General who was prepared to talk to her about her husband and his days in the Army.

Araminta rose first to kiss the General on the cheek and Caro did the same.

"Sit down, General," Lady Sinclair said as he kissed her hand. "Will you have a cup of coffee, or would you prefer a glass of madeira?"

"Coffee will suit me admirably," the General answered.

Lady Sinclair poured out the coffee and Caro added the sugar and cream.

The General glanced at Araminta meaningfully, and she realised that he had something to tell her and she must somehow find the chance to speak alone with him.

It was however not easy and only when he rose to go did she manage to say firmly:

"I will see the General downstairs. You stay with Mama, Caro."

Her sister understood and Araminta went with the General from the drawing-room down to the hall.

There Araminta led the way into the small sitting-room at the back of the house and shut the door.

"I came to see you, Araminta," the General said, "because I have a special engagement for you tomorrow evening."

Araminta waited and he went on:

"It is with Lord Rothingham, who was present at the dinner last night."

He smiled and added:

"Perhaps I should have started by telling you what you know already, that the dinner was a complete success and the Prince Regent conceded that, on that occasion at any rate, Bouvais had surpassed Carême in culinary expertise!"

"Did he .. really say that?" Araminta asked breathlessly.

"Shall I say he was browbeaten by the Marquis into saying something of the sort?"

The General's eyes twinkled as he went on:

"As you know, the Regent does not like to admit defeat and he has already decided to give a dinner at which Carême will produce dishes which have never appeared in London before."

"I can see," Araminta remarked, "that this is a contest which could go on indefinitely."

"To your advantage, my dear."

Araminta looked at him questioningly and he said:

"That is what I came to tell you. Lord Rothingham is determined to out-do the Marquis, and he has asked that you will produce a meal so unusual and exotic that it will eclipse anything that was consumed last night!"

"I think I have almost .. committed myself to stay at Wayne ..." Araminta began, remembering what the Butler had told her.

"You have not heard the end of my story," the General interrupted. "Lord Rothingham has said that if you will do what he asks tomorrow evening, when the Prince will be dining with him, he is prepared to double the fee you are already receiving!"

"Double it?" Araminta exclaimed incredulously.

"He will pay you forty guineas!"

"It cannot be true!"

"Money means nothing to men like Rothingham. They risk a thousand times that amount every night on the gaming tables. He wishes to prove to the Prince Regent that he can provide him with a better meal than Wayne did last night."

Araminta laughed.

"They are really very childish!"

"Very!" the General agreed, "especially as Rothingham and the Marquis live side by side and there has always been a good deal of rivalry between them on the race-course."

Araminta was thinking.

"Is it possible for me to do it?" she enquired.

"Only you can decide that," the General said, "But I imagine there are some dishes which your father has told you about or you have cooked for him which do not usually appear on an Englishman's table."

"Forty guineas!" Araminta said almost beneath her breath. "I cannot refuse, can I?"

"It means that you will be able to pay off Harry's debt quicker than you expected."

"Thanks entirely to you, Uncle Alex," Araminta said quickly. "You know as well as I do that I expected, if I was lucky, to receive no more than five guineas a dinner."

"Then I will tell Rothingham that you accept his offer. And by the way, he understands that you may want to spend as much again on purchasing unusual and undoubtedly expensive ingredients for your menu."

"You are very kind to me, Uncle Alex!"

"I only wish I was rich enough to help you without your having to go to all this trouble," the General said.

There was so much kindness in his voice and in the expression in his eyes that Araminta felt an impulse to tell him about Lord Yeoman.

The General would understand, he might be able to help better than she could.

Then, even as she opened her lips to speak, she heard a sound overhead and realised that either her mother or Caro was moving about in the drawing-room upstairs.

If Lady Sinclair was aware that the General was still in the house she would think it strange. Araminta went to the door of the sitting-room to say in a whisper:

"Tell Lord Rothingham I will do as he asks, but I must know by this evening how many guests he has invited."

"I will send you a note," the General replied. "The dinner is to take place before the Duchess of Beaufort's Ball."

"So it will not need to last a long time," Araminta said quickly.

"Quality, not quantity!" the General smiled. "There will also be ladies present. The Regent will be accompanied by Lady Hertford."

Araminta opened the door.

"Thank you once again, Uncle Alex," she murmured.

The General smiled at her.

Then with conspiratorial stealth he crept across the hall and Araminta let him out of the front door.

'Forty guineas!' she told herself, 'but how shall I ever think of a menu that will be worth that sort of money?'

Before she set out for Wayne House after the light luncheon they had eaten at half after noon, Araminta had told Caro what she had to do.

She begged her to busy herself immediately in making sotelties and puddings that would be fantastic enough to please Lord Rothingham.

"I will start as soon as Mama goes to lie down," Caro promised.

Then she added teasingly with a smile:

"I knew that eventually we should have to find a hundred ostriches, or search for a porcupine and the leg of a wild boar!"

"I doubt if we could procure any of those in Leadenhall Market," Araminta replied.

"Uncle Alex has been very kind, has he not?" Caro asked.

"The best friend that any of us could possibly wish for," Araminta answered in heartfelt tones.

* * * * * *

Araminta set off for Wayne House feeling so apprehensive that it was like a heavy stone within her breast. She wished now she had confided in the General.

At the same time there was really nothing he could have done.

She was sure he would merely have advised her to leave Lord Yeoman to his own devices and concern herself only with Harry's difficulties.

Wayne House seemed in the afternoon sunshine to be

even more impressive than it had looked the first time she saw it.

As she travelled down Park Lane she glanced at the house on the other side of it and saw that Lord Rothingham's mansion was not nearly so fine in appearance.

It was larger, built of dark grey stone, but there was something slightly forbidding about it, while the Grecian portico of Wayne House gave it a lightness and an elegance which was a complete contrast.

The two gardens adjoined and Araminta thought with a smile of the rivalries which existed between the two distinguished owners.

'Supposing Lord Rothingham's dinner is considered better than the Marquis's,' she thought, 'will I be asked to produce an even more superlative meal?'

It might go on indefinitely, and if her fee was doubled every time she would soon be as rich as her employers!

It was an amusing thought and Araminta was smiling as she ran down the steps which led to the basement door.

"You're early, Miss," Jim said as he opened it for her. "We weren't expecting you for several hours."

"I want to see Major Brownlow," Araminta said. "Will someone take me to him?"

"I'd ask Mr. Henson, but he's a-resting."

"Then do not disturb him," Araminta said quickly.

Jim fetched Henry, a good looking young man of eighteen who was over six feet in height, as were all the footmen employed at Wayne House.

"Major Brownlow's in his office, Miss Bouvais," he said. "If you'll come upstairs with me I'll ask him if he'll see you."

"Thank you," Araminta said.

She would have followed him but he stopped, looked at the bonnet she was wearing and said:

"Begging your pardon, Miss, but you should take your bonnet off. It's not correct for the servants to go to the front part of the house in their outdoor clothes."

"No, of course not," Araminta agreed.

She hoped there were no other *faux pas* she was likely to commit in her present position.

She took off her bonnet, smoothed her fair hair and gave the skirt of her white gown a shake.

She had made her own gown of cheap muslin and with its blue ribbon round the high waist, it was very plain. At the same time it revealed the soft curves of her slim figure.

As it was a hot day, she had carried her cloak in which she intended to return that evening, and now she laid it on a chair in the passage and put her bonnet on top of it.

When she had slipped away from Russell Square she had left Caro to explain to her mother that once again she had gone out with Harry.

"I do not know where Harry is this afternoon," she said to Caro. "We can only hope that he does not come home unexpectedly. Tell Hannah to be looking out for him and prevent him from speaking to Mama until she has warned him that he must have an explanation for my not being with him."

"I will do that," Caro promised. "I believe that Harry was not able to sell his horses yesterday at the price he hoped, and is having another try today."

"That must be the excuse," Araminta said.

As she followed Henry up the narrow steps which led from the basement she told herself that it was unlikely the Marquis would be at home at this hour.

But when Major Brownlow had finished with her, she decided, she would ask when she could see His Lordship.

When she had awakened that morning it had seemed in retrospect that the drama which had taken place the previous night with Lord Yeoman could only be a figment of her imagination.

"How could any young man be so stupid as to gamble away such an enormous fortune?" she asked herself.

Then she thought that the money Harry had lost was in proportion just as large to them.

Major Brownlow's office was on the ground floor adjacent to the Library where the Marquis always sat when he was alone.

Araminta was not aware of this, but as she waited in the passage while Henry enquired if Major Brownlow would see her she noticed the valuable pieces of furniture in the wide corridors.

She also had a glimpse in the distance of the marble hall with its pale apple green Adam walls and exquisite Grecian statuary.

There were tables of gilded wood with marble tops which she knew had been carved by the great masters of the previous century. There were Chippendale mirrors with their Chinese pagodas and exotic dragons which she thought exquisite.

Henry was some time in the office and Araminta moved to look at a picture.

It was an oil-painting of a gentleman leaning against a stone urn.

In the background was a magnificent house silhouetted against green trees with a lake in front of it.

Beneath the picture there was a plaque inscribed: *'The 1st Marquis of Wayne' by Thomas Gainsborough.*

Araminta looked at the picture with interest.

There was no doubt that the first Marquis was a handsome man and she thought that he probably was either the grandfather or the great-grandfather of the present holder of the title.

He looked proud but pleasant, and she wondered if he would have been displeased and perhaps affronted to know how many people violently disliked the present Marquis.

She was so intent on staring at the portrait that she did not notice Henry approach until he reached her side.

"I've been a long time, Miss," he said, "because th'Major was with His Lordship."

"Will he see me now?" Araminta enquired.

"His Lordship wishes to see ye, Miss. He be in th' Library. 'Tis next door."

"His Lordship?"

Araminta felt her heart give a frightened leap.

It was true she had intended to see the Marquis but not until after she had talked with Major Brownlow.

Henry was already moving ahead of her, not towards the

office outside which she had been waiting, but further along the corridor.

"There be a communicating door, between the Major's office and th'Library," Henry explained, "but I'd best announce ye formally."

Now Araminta could see a double door of carved mahogany which was very imposing.

Henry paused and looked at her, his hand going out towards the handle.

"His Lordship be in for a shock, Miss," he said with a grin. "He still thinks ye're a man."

The footman winked as he spoke. It was impertinent, but at the same time to Araminta it was somehow comforting.

Henry opened the door.

"Th' Chef, M'Lord!" he said abruptly.

Drawing a deep breath Araminta walked slowly into the room.

The Library was larger than she had expected and far more impressive. In fact, she told herself, it was the most beautiful room she had ever seen.

There were books rising from the floor to the ceiling and there were exquisitely carved gilt tables and several French commodes.

The windows were hung with red velvet curtains which picked out the colours of the Savonnerie carpet which covered the floor.

She only managed to have a quick glance round before the man who was standing at the window looking out into the sunlit garden turned round.

As he did so, Araminta heard Henry close the door behind her.

She stood just inside the room, her hair very fair against the dark walls. Her grey eyes, wide and apprehensive, seemed to fill her small, heart-shaped face.

The man standing at the window stared at her incredulously.

The Marquis was taller than Araminta had anticipated.

She had expected him to be autocratic and overwhelming, but not so good-looking.

In fact she had never seen or imagined a more handsome or indeed a more masculine-looking man.

He was exquisitely dressed in the very height of fashion, and yet his clothes, as Harry's never seemed to do, fitted him so perfectly that they were a part of himself, and he was unconscious of them.

There was, however, something hard about him which showed itself in the line of his mouth and the manner in which he carried his head.

"Who are you?"

The Marquis's voice broke the silence.

"I .. am the .. Chef .. My Lord!"

Araminta's voice in contrast sounded even to herself weak and ineffective.

"You mean you are Bouvais?"

"Yes .. My Lord."

"And you planned and prepared and cooked the dinner last night and the night before?"

"Yes .. My Lord."

"You astound me!" the Marquis exclaimed.

He moved from the window and walked towards the fireplace to stand with his back to the carved marble mantelshelf.

"Perhaps you had better sit down," he said after a moment.

"Thank you .. My Lord."

Araminta realised that this was a remarkable concession but she was wondering if her legs would hold her upright for much longer.

She moved over the soft carpet for what seemed a very long way before finally she reached the fireplace.

The Marquis indicated an upright chair with a gold-framed back and seat covered with *petit point*.

Araminta sat down on the edge of it, clasping her hands together in her lap.

Her fingers were cold and she felt her heart was fluttering wildly in her breast.

"You really are the Chef?" the Marquis asked after a moment, his eyes on her face. "This is not some jest which is being played upon me?"

97

"No .. My Lord. I cooked for .. you last night .. and I hope .. to your .. satisfaction."

"Both meals were superlative, as you well know," the Marquis answered "But how can you be so experienced and have learnt so much at your age?"

Araminta smiled.

"I have cooked for some years, My Lord .. and I was well .. taught."

"That is obvious, but .."

The Marquis paused. Then he smiled as he exclaimed:

"When His Royal Highness learns of this he really will have a stroke!"

"Then perhaps it would be .. best not to .. tell him," Araminta suggested primly.

"Who knows of your identity?" the Marquis enquired.

"Only the .. General."

"Then for the moment perhaps it would be best to keep it that way," the Marquis said. "Although I imagine such a secret will leak out sooner or later."

Araminta did not answer and after a moment the Marquis said:

"Major Brownlow intended to see you this afternoon to ask you on my instructions to stay here on a permanent basis. Would that be to your liking?"

"I am afraid not, My Lord. I would, however, be glad to stay until the end of next week with the exception of tomorrow evening."

"And why can you not be here tomorrow evening?" the Marquis enquired.

"Because the General has promised that I shall cook a dinner for Lord Rothingham."

"Dammit! I thought Rothingham was up to something last night!" the Marquis exclaimed. "You must refuse!"

"I am afraid that would not be possible," Araminta said coldly. "I have already informed the General that I will accept His Lordship's offer."

"You consider his offer was made before mine?"

"Yes, My Lord."

98

The Marquis looked annoyed and there was a frown between his eyes.

Araminta glanced at him a little apprehensively.

She had a great deal more to say and she did not wish to make him angry.

The Marquis made up his mind.

"Very well, go to Rothingham if you must, but let me make this clear. I expect you otherwise to serve me alone for as long as you are able to do so. I think too it would be wisest for you to move into the house."

"No .. I cannot do that!" Araminta said quickly. "And I can only cook for you at dinner-time."

"You cannot manage luncheon?"

Araminta shook her head.

"No, My Lord."

"I suppose because you are such a good cook you think you can dictate your own terms, however inconvenient they may be to your employer?"

There was something contemptuous in the way he spoke which annoyed her.

"As you say, I can make my own terms, My Lord. I can only express regret if they inconvenience you."

"But you do not intend to alter them to suit me?"

"No .. My Lord."

She felt the Marquis was debating whether to dispense altogether with her services because she was defying him.

'He is cruel, unkind and ruthless!' Araminto told herself. 'Even if I were able to do as he wished, I would refuse out of sheer perversity!'

She raised her chin a little and looked at the Marquis defiantly.

Her eyes met his and she felt he was attempting to compel her by sheer will-power to obey him.

Something obstinate made her determine that she would never give in to him, whatever the issue.

At the same time she thought the Marquis must hear the frightened thumping of her heart.

"Very well," he conceded finally. "I accept your terms. But I am hoping that you will find the work at Wayne House so pleasant that you will stay at least until the end of the season."

"I am afraid that will be impossible."

"Why?"

The question was sharp.

"For .. personal reasons, My Lord."

"I presume you are to be married?"

"No .. nothing like .. that," Araminta replied quickly.

"Then will you explain more fully why you cannot stay, as I wish you to do, until I leave London?"

"I am sorry .. My Lord. I can give you no .. explanation. I will try to please you until the end of next week .. then I must .. leave."

The Marquis's lips tightened and she knew he thought she was being difficult.

Because she had no wish to incense him further she said quickly in a low voice:

"Could I speak to Your Lordship on a very different matter?"

"Of course."

"When I came to cook your dinner the night before last, I brought with me a number of dishes already prepared."

"So my secretary informed me. It is unusual, but I have no objection to your making any arrangements you desire as regards your work."

"Thank you, My Lord, but it was not about that I wished to speak."

"What then?"

"While I was at supper with the rest of the staff, I left the ingredients for a *crème brûlée* on a slab in the larder."

'*Crème brûlée*," the Marquis remarked. "My favourite pudding!"

"That is what I was told afterwards," Araminta said, "and I suppose that was why when I returned to the larder after supper I found it had been poisoned!"

If she had wanted to shock the Marquis she certainly succeeded. He stared at her incredulously, before he exclaimed:

"Poisoned?"

"Yes .. My Lord. I found a cat licking the bowl which

contained the eggs and cream, and it died almost instantly!"

"Do you mean that someone intended to kill me?"

"Yes . . My Lord."

"And do you know who this person was?"

"Your late Chef, My Lord, put the poison in the bowl, but he did so on the instigation of . . someone else."

"Who?"

"Lord Yeoman!"

The Marquis stiffened, then he said:

"How do you know this? Who told you?"

"Last night when I left here," Araminta explained, "Lord Yeoman was waiting for me in the hackney carriage. He told me what he had done, and his first attempt having failed, he tried to bribe me to try again."

"Damn the young fool! I will have him arrested!" the Marquis ejaculated.

"When he knew that I would not help him in that way," Araminta went on quietly, "he told me that he intended to shoot himself. I think he might have done so if I had not prevented him."

"Do you really expect me to believe this fantastic story?" the Marquis enquired harshly.

"It is the truth," Araminta replied, "and unless a solution can be found to Lord Yeoman's problem, I am certain he will kill himself. He would rather die than ask his father and mother to sell their home, which he must do to obtain the money he owes you."

"The whole thing is preposterous!" the Marquis ejaculated. "Somebody should bring Yeoman to his senses. He had no right to threaten you or to behave in such an hysterical manner."

"He is hysterical because he is desperate! His father is in ill-health. Lord Yeoman is certain it will kill both his parents if everything has to be sold over their heads."

"That, surely, is Yeoman's problem, not yours," the Marquis remarked.

"I have made it mine," Araminta answered, "because Lord Yeoman is very young and undoubtedly very foolish."

The Marquis did not speak and she went on:

"Like many young men, he came to London to enjoy himself, but found that Your Lordship constituted a challenge which he could not resist."

"What do you mean by that?" the Marquis enquired.

"You must know that Your Lordship's high-handed manner and your reputation of always being a winner, excites the determination of the young? They want to stand up to you .. they long to defeat you .. and in trying to do so .. they destroy themselves!"

There was a throb behind Araminta's words that was unmistakable and the Marquis stared at her before he said:

"Lord Yeoman is obviously a very close friend of yours."

"I had never even .. heard of him until last .. night."

"Then why should you concern yourself so deeply with his problems?"

"Because he is young, because he is not the only young man you have bankrupted," she answered. "If he kills himself .. as I am certain he means to do .. his death will be at your .. door."

"Can you really expect me to hold myself responsible for every young fool who throws away money he has not got on a game of chance?"

"It is your fault because you .. incite them," Araminta retorted, "and because it is an .. unequal and .. unfair contest."

"What do you mean by unfair?" the Marquis asked.

"You can afford to lose. You are risking nothing that matters to you .. but they risk everything .. not only the money they do not possess .. but also their whole future and perhaps even their .. lives."

"I do not ask them to game with me," the Marquis said defensively.

"Not in so many words," Araminta replied. "But because you are so successful and everything they desire to be, they pit themselves against you. They do not realise that because you are so rich, so powerful, so autocratic, they are .. defeated even before they .. begin."

Now there was an undoubted sob in Araminta's voice.

Because she was afraid of bursting into tears, because she

felt so strongly about what she was saying, she rose to her feet to walk towards the window fighting for self-control.

The Marquis did not move but his eyes watched her, and after some moments he said quietly:

"What are you asking me to do?"

Araminta turned round.

Her eyes were misty with unshed tears and her lips were trembling a little.

"I am asking you to .. cancel Lord Yeoman's debt," she said. "It will mean very little to you .. in fact you have nothing to lose."

She drew in a deep breath.

"But if you will do this, you will not only have .. saved a very young man's .. life, but you will have shown that you can be generous and understanding .. something which .. no-one has ever known you to be."

"You are very frank, Miss Bouvais!" the Marquis said with a wry smile.

There was a pause.

"I am sorry," Araminta said in a low voice, "please forgive me if I have been .. rude."

"Shall we say frankness about myself is something I seldom hear," the Marquis answered, "and I infer from what you have said that you do not have a very high opinion of me."

"My .. opinion is of no .. consequence," Araminta said. "We were .. talking about .. Lord Yeoman."

"I have never in my whole life," the Marquis said, "and this is true, received a more extraordinary request. Perhaps I should not only grant what you ask, but also promise you that in future my opponents will be obliged to show me their birth certificate before I agree to play with them."

He was being sarcastic but Araminta's eyes lit up.

"Do you .. really mean that you will cancel Lord Yeoman's debt?" she asked breathlessly.

"You leave me little alternative," the Marquis answered. "I have either to do as you ask or condemn this young idiot to die. As you so rightly say, it would be on my conscience – if I had one."

"I think .. you have."

Araminta had walked towards him as he had been speaking and now she stood facing him looking up into his eyes.

For a moment they stared at each other, then the Marquis said slowly:

"I have a feeling if I agree to this extraordinary proposition I should make you promise to tell me about yourself."

"I .. cannot do .. that." Araminta answered.

She did not know why, but it was impossible to take her eyes from the Marquis's.

His eyes were also grey, she discovered, a paler grey than hers and steely! There was also something penetrating in the manner in which he was looking at her.

It was almost as if he stared deep into her heart. Then she told herself she was being imaginative.

'He looks so magnificent!' she thought, 'and after all, he is not as .. frightening as he .. seems. He has spared Lord Yeoman and I must be .. grateful to him.'

"Why can you not tell me about yourself?" the Marquis asked.

"There is .. nothing to .. tell."

"I know that is not true, and I am curious."

"I am .. sorry! Because you have been so .. kind. I would like to do as you .. wish but I must .. refuse."

"Why?"

It was a monosyllable he was continually snapping at her.

"Because it must remain a .. secret," she answered, "and it is not mine alone .. but somebody .. else's."

She spoke a little self-consciously because she was nervous, and now her eyes dropped before his. Her eye-lashes were very dark against her pale cheeks.

The Marquis did not speak and after a moment Araminta said nervously:

"I think I should .. return to the .. kitchen. I do not know how many people you have dining here tonight but there is .. nothing prepared."

"I will make a bargain with you," the Marquis said.

"A .. bargain?" Araminta asked nervously.

She looked up at him again.

"It is quite a fair one," he said reassuringly. "I will find Lord Yeoman, tell him that his debt is cancelled and send him back to the country. He must grow up before he enters a card-room again."

Araminta clasped her hands together.

"That would be very wonderful of .. you! Lord Yeoman is at White's. He is waiting for me to send him a message."

"I will see him myself," the Marquis said. "that is if you will fulfil your part of the bargain."

"What do you .. want me to .. do?" Araminta asked.

"I want you to cook a dinner tonight for me alone," the Marquis said, "and after dinner I want you to join me so that we can talk for a little while. Is that too much to ask?"

"No .." Araminta said doubtfully. "I .. suppose not."

"But you would rather not do it?"

"It is not .. that," she replied. "It is just that .. I .. never .."

She was about to say that she had never been alone with a man. Then she remembered who she was supposed to be.

A Chef would hardly ask for a chaperon and the Marquis would not understand her hesitation.

At the same time it was very unconventional, and for the Marquis to entertain one of his own servants would arouse a great deal of comment below stairs.

As if he knew what she was thinking the Marquis said:

"You are quite right. We should not talk together here. Will you allow me to take you out to supper? There are places where we can talk and drink a glass of champagne without being disturbed."

'Mama would be horrified!' Araminta thought to herself.

Then she remembered that her mother would never know, and if she could save Lord Yeoman on these terms, it was almost impossible to refuse.

The Marquis's eyes were on her face and as if he was aware of her indecision he said quietly:

"You can trust me not to keep you any longer than you wish to stay."

"Then .. thank you .. My Lord. I shall be .. pleased to do as you .. suggest."

She curtsied and turned towards the door.

Only as she had nearly reached it did she hesitate, turn and look back.

The Marquis was standing where she had left him and his eyes were on her.

"I .. hope Your Lordship .. realises," she said in a low voice, "that I shall only be able to come .. dressed as I am now .. and you might be .. ashamed of my appearance."

"I shall not be ashamed," the Marquis said. "But so that you will not feel embarrassed we will go somewhere very quiet."

"Thank you, My Lord."

Araminta curtsied again and opened the door.

Only as she stepped outside did she feel as if she had been thrown into a tempestuous sea, yet by some miracle had escaped being drowned.

CHAPTER FIVE

Through the window Araminta could see a brightly lighted doorway and a powdered footman opening the door of the carriage ahead of them.

"It looks very grand!" she said apprehensively.

The Marquis sitting beside her smiled.

"There is no need for you to be nervous," he said. "We shall not be seen."

Araminta did not understand what he meant until entering the large rather garish hallway they were shown up a wide staircase to the first floor.

There was a long corridor with doors opening off each side of it. The man who escorted them opened one and, speaking with a foreign accent, said:

"I hope this'll be to Your Lordship's liking."

"It will do," the Marquis said briefly.

"I'll send the maître d'hôtel to you immediately, M'Lord."

The man, bowing ingratiatingly, shut the door behind him.

Araminta looked round at first apprehensively, then surprised at what she saw.

It was a small, square room decorated with a flamboyant wallpaper and hung with tasselled curtains of ruby red velvet.

The lights were shaded, there was a large, comfortable sofa covered with silk cushions at the far side of the room and in the centre there was a table laid with a lace tablecloth and lit by two candles.

She turned her face to the Marquis as if asking for an explanation.

"As I told you," he said quietly, "we will not be seen."

"But I thought this would be a restaurant."

"It is one," he replied, 'and kept by a Chef of whom I think you will approve; but a customer can also obtain, as you see, a *cabinet particulier,* or private room."

"It seems rather .. strange," Araminta said as if speaking to herself.

As they came up the stairs she had heard voices in the distance and the sound of music.

She was sure there were a great number of people downstairs, perhaps in the large restaurant, such as she had been too nervous to enter.

At any rate, she thought, here alone with the Marquis she need not be ashamed of her plain gown.

She unfastened her cloak, the Marquis took it from her and laid it on a chair by the door.

After she had finished cooking his dinner at Wayne House, Araminta had asked if she could wash and had been taken to an empty bed-room in the basement.

It was sparsely furnished but clean, and there was a washhand basin and a mirror in which she could arrange her hair.

She washed carefully and wished after she had done so that she had a smart, exciting gown to wear.

She had indeed put on her best dress before leaving home since she intended to speak to him that afternoon.

But she was well aware that she would look very dowdy beside the ladies the Marquis must usually entertain either in his own home or elsewhere.

'Anyway, what does it matter what I look like?' Araminta asked herself. 'He has only brought me here because, having given in over Lord Yeoman, he feels he has to exact some sort of penalty from me.'

At the same time something irrepressibly feminine within her longed to make him admire her as a woman.

She was surprised at her feelings where he was concerned.

She had hated him so fervently because of what he had done to Harry, and she had been prepared to fight him and to go on fighting him with regard to Lord Yeoman.

She could hardly believe that he had capitulated so easily

or that she had in fact saved at least one young man from paying for the consequences of his stupidity.

She was quite certain that the Marquis would insist, as he had said he would, on Lord Yeoman returning to the country and his parents.

But anyway he would have learnt his lesson and never again would he behave in such an irresponsible and idiotic manner.

'The Marquis has been very kind and I must show him that I am grateful,' Araminta thought.

A footman had come to the kitchen after dinner to say with a note of surprise in his voice:

"The Master says he's going your way, Miss, and'll take you home in his carriage."

"That is very gracious of His Lordship," Araminta replied coolly.

But she was well aware that the kitchen staff looked after her enquiringly as she left them to climb the stairs from the basement to the ground floor.

Henson came forward as she appeared and said in what she thought was a disapproving tone:

"His Lordship's not quite ready, Miss Bouvais. You'd best get into the carriage so that you'll not keep him waiting."

"I will do that, Mr. Henson."

A closed carriage, embellished with the Marquis's coat-of-arms, was waiting outside the front door.

Araminta had only just seated herself when she saw him come into the lighted hall.

It was impossible for her not to be overwhelmed by his appearance.

Araminta had seen her father and various of their neighbours in the country wearing evening-dress, but there was no comparison between their appearance and that of the Marquis.

Never had she imagined that a man could look so magnificent and at the same time so distinguished.

His hair was cut in the wind-swept style which had been brought into fashion by the Regent and immortalised by Lawrence's portrait of him.

The Marquis's spotless cravat against his firm chin was an intricate triumph, and his cut-away coat with its long tails fitted as if it were a second skin.

'Why have I not a beautiful gown to wear?' Araminta found herself wishing.

The reason was that the money she might have expended on some becoming and fashionable garment was in fact owed to the Marquis himself!

'If only he knew how I am suffering because of him!' she thought.

Then with an effort at being sensible she forced herself to remember that their relationship was that of employer and servant, and the way she looked or did not look would not concern him.

She was however again very conscious of her appearance when she no longer wore the concealing cloak, and the Marquis, in his magnificence, seemed to fill the whole room until it was difficult to look at anything else.

"Are there a lot of rooms like this?" Araminta asked.

Feeling shy and unable to meet his eyes, at the same time she felt obliged to say something.

"Quite a number," the Marquis answered, "and they are very much in demand."

"By whom?" Araminta enquired curiously.

"By people who, like ourselves, do not wish to be seen," the Marquis replied. "I imagine that the majority of users are married men who wish to entertain a pretty lady without their wives being aware of it."

Araminta did not answer and after a moment he said:

"You look as if the idea shocks you."

"I am not really .. shocked," Araminta answered. "I am surprised! I suppose, because my father and mother were so happy together, I did not realise there were men who wished to deceive their wives in such a way."

The Marquis pulled out a chair at the table and Araminta sat down in it.

As she did so the door opened and a waiter appeared with a menu.

The Marquis took it from him.

"Have you had anything to eat this evening?" he asked Araminta.

She shook her head.

She had been both too anxious about cooking a dinner to his liking and also, in some way she could not explain, too excited about what lay ahead to feel in the least hungry.

"Then I must insist that you try some of the specialities for which Louis is famous. Shall I order for you?"

"Yes, please," Araminta answered. "But I am not very hungry."

The Marquis gave an order in fluent French and the waiter bowed his way from the room.

"Who is Louis?" Araminta asked.

"He is a Frenchman who came to England and opened this place which has been a great success."

"I heard that many Chefs had left France after the Revolution and during the war," Araminta said.

"Louis is one of them," the Marquis replied. "He used to work for the *Duc* de Chamois. If the *Duc* is still living, which I somewhat doubt, he certainly could not now afford the services of such an expensive Chef!"

He paused, then added with a smile:

"He is considered to be a Master of his art, but may I say that I do not consider him to be in the same category as yourself?"

"Thank you."

"I enjoyed my dinner tonight."

"I am glad."

She had in fact been a little worried in case he thought the meal too plain.

The meat that she found in the larder was, in Araminta's estimation, not good enough, but a great hamper of chickens, eggs and vegetables had arrived that very day from the country.

They had formed the nucleus of the dinner which had finished with a *crème brûlée*, despite the fact that Araminta felt that for the Marquis it might hold unpleasant associations.

"I shall find it very difficult to eat anything more," the Marquis said, "but I want you to enjoy yourself and forget your work."

The table was small and he seated himself beside Araminta instead of opposite.

She looked up at him and felt as she had in the carriage that he was very near and it made her tinglingly aware of him.

"What is your Christian name?" he asked.

"Araminta."

"Unusual and lovely!"

Araminta blushed.

"You were telling me that you were surprised that gentlemen should come to a place like this," the Marquis said. "Surely you must be aware that most marriages are unhappy?"

"I am sure that is not true," Araminta replied, "except perhaps in .. London."

"You think in the country it is different?"

"I am sure it is," she answered. "Gentlemen who live in the country have not so many idle hours to fill that they must waste them at the gambling tables or perhaps with women other than their wives."

She spoke positively but there was a mocking note in the Marquis's voice as he answered:

"You are very scathing, and of course intolerant, which is a characteristic of youth."

"Perhaps what you are really saying is that our standards are higher because we have not yet been disillusioned."

"That may be the explanation," the Marquis agreed. "It is certainly many years since I had any illusions."

Araminta wondered to herself if this was the explanation for what Harry and Lord Yeoman had described as his aloof, contemptuous attitude.

The waiter brought them a bottle of champagne surrounded by ice in a silver cooler.

He poured a little into the Marquis's glass who tasted it, approved and the waiter filled Araminta's glass.

"Do you like champagne?" the Marquis asked.

"I have seldom drunk it," she answered, "except on special occasions, like a birthday or Christmas."

She thought the Marquis might be surprised, and added:

"My father preferred claret, and anyhow we could not often afford such luxuries."

"Your family is poor?"

"Very poor by your standards."

"I am sure you are not strong enough to work as hard as you are doing at the moment," the Marquis said.

"It is tiring," Araminta admitted, "but I can manage."

"As I said, I think it is too much for you."

"I .. I shall not have to .. work so hard when I leave at the end of the week."

"Where are you going?"

She gave the Marquis a quick glance, as if she realised this was a question which might trap her, and replied evasively:

"To the .. country."

"And you are not to be married?"

"I have already told you that I am not."

"And yet many men must have asked you."

Araminta laughed.

"I can answer that quite truthfully .. no-one!"

"Then you must live on a desert island," the Marquis said, "or else in a county where every man is blind!"

Araminta would have laughed again, but she met his eyes and somehow the sound died on her lips.

"You are very beautiful, Araminta!" the Marquis said softly.

She was aware that he had used her Christian name for the first time; but it was not only that, it was the expression in his grey eyes which made her suddenly feel unsure and a little frightened, although she was uncertain why.

It was with relief that she realised the waiter was bringing in the food.

A consommé which was clear and golden was followed by a dish which Araminta looked at curiously.

"It is called 'Poulet Suprême Louis'," the Marquis explained, "and is a great speciality of the Proprietor's. I shall be interested to see what you think of it."

113

He himself was not eating but playing with a few black olives and some nuts which had been placed on the table in front of him.

Araminta tasted the chicken dish.

"It is very good!"

"Which is high praise from you!" the Marquis smiled.

"The only criticism I have to make is that it has been wrongly named."

The Marquis raised his eye-brows.

"It should not be called '*Poulet Suprême Louis*'. The first word should be 'Lapin'."

"Rabbit!" the Marquis exclaimed. "The old scoundrel! but very few people would know the difference, and rabbit is of course very much cheaper than chicken."

He laughed.

"I shall send for Louis, and see his face when I tell him his deception has been discovered!"

"No .. please," Araminta said quickly. "I would not wish you to do that. It would be embarrassing and, as you say, very few people would know the difference."

She thought the Marquis would argue with her and she pleaded again:

"Please .."

"I will not do anything that you do not wish me to do," the Marquis said. "Although I must say, Araminta, you are having a very strange effect upon me."

"In what way?" she asked curiously.

"I do not remember ever before allowing my intentions to be changed or interrupted by a woman," he said. "Now in the space of a few hours I find my determination undermined and my wishes circumvented."

"I feel I have not thanked you enough for your .. kindness where Lord Yeoman is .. concerned," Araminta said. "Was he very surprised?"

"He was astounded!" the Marquis replied. "And he asked me to express to you his deepest and most heartfelt gratitude."

"And he is returning to the country?"

"I made it a condition of my cancelling his debt."

"I thought you would."

"Why were you so certain I would do so?"

"I had a feeling that you would try to explain away your . . generosity by extracting from him some concession in . . return."

"As I have extracted one from you!" the Marquis said.

"It was not very . . hard for me to comply with what you . . asked."

"But I had the feeling that you were reluctant because it was unconventional for you to have supper with me."

"It is . . something I have never done . . before."

"You have never eaten a meal alone with a man?"

"No!"

"And you tell me no young man has ever proposed to you?"

She shook her head.

"And you have never been kissed?"

Araminta gave a little start and the colour rose in her cheeks.

"No . . of course . . not!" she said quickly.

"You are very young," the Marquis remarked, "and yet you have a knowledge of cooking that might be envied by a man or woman twenty years your senior! I cannot understand how it has happened."

"You said we would not talk of my work," Araminta reminded him.

"You make it very difficult for me not to be curious about you," the Marquis replied. "Once again, Araminta, you are trying to prevent me from doing what I wish to do."

"What is . . that?"

"Getting to know you better and trying to understand why you are what you are."

"I would much rather we talked about . . you."

"It is a subject I find infinitely boring," the Marquis answered, "but I am prepared to be fair. What particularly do you want to ask me?"

Araminta looked at him.

He was sitting back in his chair, holding a glass of champagne in his hand and very much at his ease.

It was difficult to understand, she thought, why when he talked to her she felt as if her heart was turning over in her breast, and when he paid her compliments her throat was constricted.

"I think I should like to know .. why you stand .. apart from life as if you were on a .. mountain and everyone else was in the .. valley below," she said at length.

The Marquis looked startled, then he sat upright.

"Who has been talking about me to you?"

"No-one particularly," Araminta replied. "It is just that I always heard you were .. aloof and somehow .. different from other men, and that is what I .. feel about you .. myself."

"Why should you feel that?"

There was a pause before Araminta answered slowly:

"It is not because you look so magnificent in appearance, and it is not because you are rich and powerful. I think the .. impression you give comes from your .. mind."

She knew the Marquis was listening and she made a little gesture with her hands.

"I am explaining myself very badly."

"And you find it unpleasant?" the Marquis asked sharply.

"No .. not in the least unpleasant," Araminta replied. "A little .. frightening, but intriguing and, as I have already said, it makes you .. different from other men."

"Everything about you bewilders me!" the Marquis ejaculated. "How old are you?"

"I am nearly nineteen."

"I can assure you, Araminta, that if I am different from other men, then you are very different from any other young woman of your age."

"Am I?" Araminta asked. "I hope not!"

"Why should you hope that?" the Marquis enquired.

"Because I would want them ..."

She stopped suddenly.

She realised that, intent on what she was saying to the Marquis, she had spoken inadvertently as if she would be associating in London with other débutantes.

Just for that second she had forgotten that there was no

future for her in the social world and that at the end of the week she was returning to the dullness of Bedfordshire.

There she would encounter only the neighbours they had known for years.

"You were saying?" the Marquis prompted.

"It is of no importance," Araminta replied, "and once again we are talking about me, not about . . you!"

"I asked you a question," the Marquis said, "and you have answered it in a manner which I find surprising."

"May I ask you another?" Araminta enquired.

"I suppose so," he conceded.

"Then why should you, with all your talents, waste your time winning money by gambling which you do not need and which can in fact make no difference to your life?"

The Marquis paused before he replied:

"It is one way of passing the time."

"But why should you want to pass it in such an idiotic manner, when there are so many other things for someone as intelligent and distinguished as you to do?"

"What are you suggesting?" the Marquis asked.

"You have an Estate in the country," Araminta replied. "Surely you have realised the terrible depression which has hit the farming industry since the end of the war?"

She saw the surprise in the Marquis's expression as she went on:

"History tells us that it is always the same after a war. The farmers who were a vital necessity while hostilities were taking place are quickly forgotten, and food imported from abroad is cheaper than that which is home-grown."

Araminta's voice deepened as she said:

"Many of the farm-labourers have been dismissed and are starving. The country banks have either gone bankrupt or will not grant any further loans. Surely someone should speak for these people and make the Government aware of their misery?"

The Marquis put his glass of champagne down on the table.

"How do you know all this?"

"Because I live in the country," Araminta replied. "I talk

to the local farmers. I see what is happening when their crops are ploughed back into the soil."

She did not add that Bedfordshire was a county which produced most of the vegetables that she had seen for sale in Covent Garden.

She had also heard her father predict before he died what would happen to the farmers, and those she had known ever since she had been a child were always glad to have someone sympathetic to listen to their complaints.

"I find the House of Lords extremely dull," the Marquis remarked at length and as if he must defend himself.

"But surely it is more interesting to gamble with human beings than a pack of cards?" Araminta asked scornfully.

A waiter entered to remove the dishes.

He poured out two cups of coffee and brought the Marquis a liqueur brandy.

Then to Araminta's surprise he went round the room dimming all the lights except for one shaded candelabrum by the big sofa and the others on the table.

He departed closing the door quietly behind him.

Araminta suddenly felt strange and a little uncomfortable.

She felt as if the shadows were menacing and the light on the cushion-covered sofa was an invitation which she did not understand.

She had hardly touched her champagne, but now she took a little sip and said nervously:

"It must be getting .. late. I think I should go .. home."

"The evening is still very young," the Marquis replied, "and there is a great deal more I wish to say to you, Araminta."

"It may sound .. rude," she said slowly, "but I have a .. feeling that I ought not to be here .. alone with you."

"What makes you feel like that?" the Marquis asked.

"I have never been to a restaurant before," Araminta confessed, "although of course I have heard of them. But I did not think they were like this .. as you said this is .. a secret place where people .. come who do not .. wish to be .. seen.'

"Do you think we are doing anything wrong?" the Marquis asked.

"No .. but perhaps if people .. knew we were here .. they would think it .. wrong for you to be .. entertaining me."

"I assure you, anyone I know would think I was extremely lucky to be with someone so beautiful and attractive."

There was something in the way the Marquis spoke which made Araminta feel that it was not the manner he would have spoken to her if he had met her socially in her mother's drawing-room.

She felt as if the walls of the room were closing in on her, and she had the insistent feeling that she must escape while she could.

She pushed back her chair and rose to her feet.

"I am very grateful to you, My Lord, for being so kind about Lord Yeoman. I have now fulfilled my part of the bargain, so .. please .. may I go .. home?"

"Suppose I say that you must stay here a little longer and that I will not let you leave me?" the Marquis asked.

Araminta felt as if her heart stopped beating.

She looked up at him and saw an expression in his eyes which made her draw in her breath. Then lifting her chin, she said quietly:

"You promised that you would not make me .. stay if I did not wish to do so. I must .. My Lord, hold you to your .. promise."

"Ever since we met you have had everything your own way," the Marquis answered. "Surely it is now my turn?"

He had not risen from his seat, and yet Araminta felt as if he towered over her. She thought there was a glint of fire in his eyes, but it might have been a trick of the candlelight.

"P . please," she said. "I do not .. like this place. There is .. something about it .. a feeling I cannot explain .. but I know I should not be .. here."

She thought the Marquis would argue with her, then suddenly he smiled.

"You are right, Araminta," he said. "It is not a suitable background for you, but there was nowhere else I could take you where we could be alone."

He rose and picked up her cloak from the chair near the door and put it round her shoulders.

Just for a moment his hands rested on her as if he held her prisoner. Then he said:

"May I add to your other attributes that you are exceedingly skilful in extricating yourself from a difficult situation?"

Araminta did not understand what he meant, and as he released her she moved towards the door.

He opened it for her and they stepped out into the corridor.

As they walked down the stairs the noise and the music was almost deafening. On reaching the front hall the Marquis took Araminta's arm and guided her out onto the steps.

A linkman fetched the Marquis's carriage and only as they stepped inside and the footman waited did Araminta realise that if he took her home he would then know where she lived.

"What is your address?" the Marquis asked.

Araminta hesitated for a moment, before she said:

"I am staying at 36 Russell Square."

It was she knew, on the opposite side of the Square to the Duke's house.

As the footman shut the door she wondered how she could prevent the Marquis from knowing she was unable to let herself in.

"You are staying with friends?" he asked.

"Until the end of the week," Araminta answered.

"I hope they look after you properly. London can be a dangerous place for anyone as lovely as you."

"Everyone has been very .. kind."

"As I have?"

"I have already told Your Lordship how grateful I am to you."

"And you enjoyed yourself this evening, even though you would not stay any longer?"

"I .. enjoyed talking to you," Araminta said, "but Your Lordship must realise it is something which must not .. happen again."

"Why not?"

She hesitated.

It would be easy to say it was because she was in his employment and the servants would think it very strange. But if she gave that explanation she would not be entirely honest.

There was something deeper than that; something which told her that she must not become too involved with him. Yet already she had the feeling she was walking on quicksands.

As if once again he knew what she was thinking, the Marquis said:

"Do you really believe that this is the last time we would wish to talk to each other? I have a feeling, Araminta, that your voice will haunt me."

She did not answer and after a moment he said:

"You have given me a great deal to think about. You have surprised and bewildered, and may I also say beguiled me in a manner which I have never experienced before?"

She glanced at him quickly and looked away again because she found he was somehow nearer to her than she had expected.

She felt a strange feeling she could not understand run through her because he was sitting at her side and because when the carriage turned a corner her shoulders touched his.

"I shall see you again, Araminta," he said. "That is something of which you may be completely certain!"

"Your .. household will .. gossip," Araminta said in a low voice.

"Let them!"

"It would be a .. mistake."

"Not a mistake for me," the Marquis answered, "and I am thinking of myself. If you wish me to alter my way of life, you can hardly suggest drastic changes then put them out of your mind as if they were not of the least consequence."

"Are you going to do as I .. suggested .. about the farmers .. I mean,"

"Shall I promise you that I will study the subject? But I want to talk to you about it. I fail to see why I should fall in with your ideas if you refuse to discuss them with me."

"You must .. realise that it is .. difficult," Araminta murmured.

"The only difficulties are made by you," the Marquis retorted. "As far as I am concerned everything is perfectly straightforward! I want to see you again, Araminta, and what is more, I intend to do so!"

She drew in her breath at the firmness with which he spoke.

They drove on in silence, and yet she had the feeling, although he did not move, that he was nearer to her than he had been before.

She almost felt as if he was encircling her with his arms and drawing her closer to him in a manner she could not understand.

He seemed overpowering and overwhelming, and yet she was not really afraid, only strangely excited in a manner she had never known before.

The carriage came to a standstill far sooner than she expected and she thought the restaurant must have been nearer to Russell Square than it had been to Park Lane.

She glanced through the window and saw they were, as she expected, on the opposite side of the Square to number three.

"Shall the footman ring the bell?" the Marquis asked.

"No! no! Everyone will be .. asleep! I have a key."

The footman opened the carriage door and the Marquis stepped out to assist Araminta to alight.

Deliberately she held onto his hand as she said:

"Goodnight, My Lord, and thank you very much!"

He bent his head and kissed her fingers.

His lips only brushed her skin, but she felt as if they burnt their way into her mind.

Then with a swift movement she ran not up the steps of the house, but through the iron gate and down the steps which led to the basement.

She was certain that the Marquis would not follow her and after a moment she heard the carriage door close and the horses start off.

She waited until she was quite certain she would not be seen, then she walked up the basement steps.

The Square was empty but she felt as if he was still beside her.

'He is haunting me!' she thought in a sudden panic.

She started to run, but even as she did so, she knew there was no escape.

. . . . . .

Very early next morning Araminta set off to the markets.

She had awakened Hannah when she had arrived back the night before and told her what she had decided to buy for Lord Rothingham's dinner.

"The General left a message here this afternoon," Hannah said. "There will be twenty to dine and they will be eating early."

"I have been planning some of the dishes," Araminta said, "but we may have to change the menu, Hannah, when we see what is for sale."

It was fortunate, however, that the majority of the goods Araminta wanted were obtainable.

Lord Rothingham had asked for exotic and unusual dishes and she thought with a little smile that when the menu was complete he would certainly not complain about its being too ordinary.

"I know what Papa would say to your menu," Caro exclaimed when she saw what Araminta had bought.

"What would he say?" Araminta asked.

"That you are providing a vulgar extravaganza for gluttons!"

Araminta laughed.

"That is exactly what I am doing! I have never met Lord Rothingham, but he sounds a stupid man who is merely jealous of his next-door neighbour!"

"Well, you have certainly spent a lot of his money," Caro remarked.

"I am sure he is the type who thinks that the more he spends the better he is served!" Araminta said scornfully.

The shopping took longer than she and Hannah had expected owing to the fact that Araminta wished to buy real Russian caviar and they had to go to several different places before they could obtain what they required.

This meant that Lady Sinclair had enquired for both Hannah and Araminta before they returned and Caro had been forced to explain that they were not in the house.

"Where could you have been, dearest?" Lady Sinclair asked when Araminta finally appeared.

Fortunately she had an answer ready.

"Did Caro not tell you, Mama?" she asked, "that Harry is giving a dinner-party to-night in his lodgings and I have promised to cook some of the dishes for him."

Lady Sinclair looked surprised and Araminta went on:

"It was much cheaper for Hannah and me to buy what was required in the markets. I feel sure you will understand that, Mama."

"Of course," Lady Sinclair said, "I expect Harry finds it difficult to pay the expensive prices that are asked in the Mayfair shops."

"I am sure he does!" Araminta agreed.

Caro had managed, Araminta found, to make a soteltie which she was certain would intrigue Lord Rothingham's guests and delight the Prince Regent.

In her usual skilful manner she had produced an enormous coloured and gilded Royal crown and around it were represented all the hobbies in which His Royal Highness was most interested.

There was a tiny white sugar replica of the Pavilion at Brighton, pictures in gingerbread frames, colourful *objets d'art* which had easily been fashioned in marzipan.

A real masterpiece on Caro's part was several little Greek goddesses wearing only the classical drapery to hide their nakedness.

"Caro you are a genius!" Araminta exclaimed in admiration. "If Lord Rothingham is not pleased with that, then he will be pleased with nothing!"

"I worked at it last night until I feel asleep at the table," Caro said, "then I started again this morning a few minutes after you and Hannah had left for the market."

"It is quite perfect!" Araminta said. "I only hope it does not get damaged when we take it to Park Lane."

"It is stronger than it looks."

"If we had enough money you should have lessons in sculpture. I am sure you could make a fortune!"

"I can hardly do that with sugar!" Caro replied, "and we certainly cannot afford any other materials for me to work with."

Araminta put her arms round her younger sister and held her close.

She wished she could meet someone wealthy so that she could help Caro.

But Harry's predicament had dampened all their hopes and she was not the only one who had to suffer because of his stupidity.

"I am sorry, Caro," she said simply and knew her sister understood.

．　．　．　．　．　．

Araminta felt unduly apprehensive about going to Lord Rothingham's.

She had become used to the servants at Wayne House and she felt anxious at having to start all over again.

She soon found there was a good reason for her apprehension.

Not only were the kitchens dark and stuffy and the equipment old-fashioned, but the place was none too clean, and the staff were surly and unco-operative.

She found on arrival that the Chef had not left, as Gustave had, but had merely been told to watch her and try and learn how to improve his own cooking.

That in itself, Araminta realised, did not create a very good atmosphere.

What was more, she found it difficult to do her best when she was surrounded by servants who resented her.

She tried to be charming, but the Chef was obviously disgruntled at being confronted by someone so young and a woman at that!

While the pantry-boys and the footmen were quite eager to be of assistance, the kitchen and scullery-maids were sulky and, in Araminta's opinion, almost half-witted.

Fortunately she and Hannah had done so much work beforehand that there was little left to do except the final cooking.

The staff could not help exclaiming over Caro's soteltie, and when the footmen carried it upstairs they told her that it looked very dramatic as the centre-piece on the dining-room table.

The floral decorations were all to be of orchids which seemed to Araminta to be appropriate.

The dishes on which she arranged the food were of gold and the guests too ate off gold-plate.

Araminta made *Blinis* – little pancakes – for the caviar and knew that one course at least needed very little cooking.

She had, however, with Hannah's help made what she always thought of as the ultimate achievement in cooking.

It was usually made, her father had told her, with game birds, but because these were not in season, Araminta had bought in Leadenhall Market a young turkey.

Into this she had put a goose, into the goose a guinea-fowl, into the guinea-fowl a pigeon and into the pigeon a quail.

It was the first time that Araminta had attempted this dish and when it was finished she felt it was a culinary triumph.

The gold plate on which the turkey stood was decorated with truffles, oysters fried Chinese fashion and stuffed mushrooms, and the whole was decorated in a manner which was a delight to the eye.

It was not easy to find ingredients for the fantastic dishes which Lord Rothingham had demanded.

But having decided on ortalans wrapped in vine leaves and wild duck with cherries cooked in red wine, Araminta added a dish which she thought might in fact annoy rather than please His Lordship.

At the same time it appealed to her sense of humour that she could fulfil his desire for something unusual, if nothing else.

"What is that?" Caro had asked, before Araminta left home.

She was looking into the bowl in which there was meat,

salted and garnished with vegetables as if it was a *pot-au-feu*.

"Guess!" Araminta replied.

"I really have no idea!" Caro said, "but I see that you have a Madeira sauce with it."

"It is called *'Oreilles a la Rouennaise'*," Araminta told her.

"Orielles?" Caro repeated. "You cannot mean – pig's ears?"

She saw by Araminta's expression it was the truth.

"But you cannot serve that to the Prince Regent!" she gasped.

"I intend to do so," Araminta said. "There are no peacocks available, I do not think a swan is worth eating, and the only ostriches in London are in the Zoo!"

Caro dissolved into laughter.

"Pig's ears! You are incorrigible! I am certain that after this Lord Rothingham will never ask you to cook for him again!"

"I shall be able to refuse if he does do so," Araminta replied. "I am engaged until the end of the week by the Marquis."

"Until Harry has paid his debt?" Caro said, and now her voice was serious.

"Exactly!" Araminta agreed.

After that, she told herself, she would never see the Marquis again.

She wondered why the thought of it was so disturbing.

CHAPTER SIX

Araminta picked up her reticule which she had placed on top of her cloak and attached the silk ribbons to her wrist.

It already contained the money which she had expended on purchasing the food for Lord Rothingham's dinner, but her fee had not been sent downstairs with it.

There was nothing more to do because the kitchen-maids had washed all the dishes which she had brought with her. They were ready to be carried to a hackney carriage as soon as she asked one of the pantry-boys to find her one.

She had learnt from the footman that Lord Rothingham's party had already left for the Duchess of Beaufort's ball.

"His Royal Highness enjoyed th'dinner, Miss," one of the footmen said. "He sampled every dish that was offered to him."

"I am glad to hear that," Araminta replied.

She saw now the same footman advancing towards her down the passage.

"I wonder," she asked tentatively, "if you would be kind enough to ask His Lordship's secretary if I might have the fee I am owed so that I may go home?"

"Me orders, Miss, were to take you upstairs when you asks for it," the footman answered.

Araminta looked at him in surprise.

However, she thought, perhaps Lord Rothingham's secretary, unlike Major Brownlow, was not prepared to entrust the servants with so much money.

All the time she had been cooking in the dark, scruffy kitchen she had told herself that it was worth it because the £40 she would receive would make so much difference to Harry.

"Will the secretary see me now?" she asked the footman.

"I expect so," he replied. "I'll show you th'way."

He went ahead of her and Araminta thought that the sooner she was free of the house the better she would be pleased.

She realised now how uncomfortable it could be to work as a servant, and it was with a sense of relief that she realised that after the end of the week she need never be forced into such a position again.

They reached the top of the stairs and she saw that, unlike those of Wayne House, the corridors were narrow and badly lit, while the furniture, though impressive, had not the quality of that which belonged to the Marquis.

Araminta however was not particularly interested in Lord Rothingham's possessions.

She felt tired and all she wanted was to receive what was her due and to return home as quickly as possible.

The footman stopped.

"This be where I were told to bring you, Miss," he said and opened the door.

Araminta entered the room and saw that it was not the secretary's office but in fact a sitting-room.

At the end of it, his back to the mantelpiece, was standing a man who she knew without being told was Lord Rothingham.

He was just as she had imagined him: about forty and florid, he was dressed in the height of fashion, wearing on his evening-coat a number of jewelled decorations.

She looked at him in surprise and he said in a voice which she instantly disliked:

"Come in, Miss Bouvais. As you see, I have waited behind to meet you."

Araminta moved slowly across the room towards him.

As she drew nearer she saw that he had protruding eyes with heavy lines beneath them which gave him a look of debauchery.

"I was right!" he said as she reached the hearth-rug. "You are even lovelier than you appeared in the distance!"

Araminta looked at him in surprise.

"In the distance, My Lord?"

"I saw you," said Lord Rothingham with a smile, "from one of my windows as you entered the side-door of Wayne House."

Araminta did not reply and Lord Rothingham continued:

"I have been told that my neighbour had an exceedingly attractive young Chef who was, incredible though it seemed, not a man, but a woman!"

There was a pause. Lord Rothingham's eyes were on Araminta's face.

"Who .. could have .. told you .. such a thing?" she asked, because she felt she must say something.

"Servants talk, my dear," Lord Rothingham replied, "and as it happens, one of my footmen is 'walking out' – if that is the right term – with one of the noble Marquis's kitchen-maids."

He gave a short laugh which was unpleasant.

"You must be aware that you have caused quite a stir in Wayne House, and I have to admit that your cooking is superb!"

"I am glad it pleased you, My Lord."

"I therefore felt in the circumstances that you should receive your reward from my own hands."

Lord Rothingham held out an envelope as he spoke and Araminta took it from him thinking that now it was in her possession she could go.

"Thank you, My Lord."

She put the envelope into her reticule.

"You are not going to open it?" Lord Rothingham asked.

"Surely there is no need?" Araminta answered. "The General informed me of what you said you would pay."

"I have fulfilled my obligations," Lord Rothingham replied, "but I have also given you a little extra – ten guineas – because I felt you deserved it."

"That is kind of you, My Lord," Araminta said, "but it is quite unnecessary. I was very satisfied with the £40 which you offered in the first place."

She told herself as she spoke that she should take the extra money out of the envelope and give it back to him.

However advantageous it might be to receive more on

Harry's behalf, she had a violent dislike, which she could not explain, of accepting any extra money from Lord Rothingham.

"I thought it would please you," he said, "and I hoped that you would be a little grateful."

"I am .. grateful, My Lord. Thank you .. very much."

"That is not a very generous way of thanking me," Lord Rothingham said.

There was a note in his voice which spelt danger and Araminta curtsied.

"Thank you .. again, My Lord, and now .. if you will excuse me .. I must be returning home."

"Not so fast!" Lord Rothingham answered. "Surely you owe me something? Not only for my generous *pourboire,* but also because I am missing the Duchess's Ball on your behalf."

"I must .. go," Araminta said quickly.

She would have turned towards the door, but Lord Rothingham put out his hand and caught her wrist.

"There is no hurry!" he said. "You are very lovely, my dear, and in fact I have been thinking about you ever since I first saw you."

Araminta tried to pull herself free of his fingers but they held her prisoner.

"Please .. let me .. go, My Lord."

She spoke in what she meant to be a cold and dignified manner, but in fact her voice sounded frightened and rather breathless.

"You must learn to reciprocate kindness with kindness," Lord Rothingham said.

Now he pulled her towards him and his other arm went round her.

Araminta began to struggle.

He was much stronger than she expected and although she fought against him he dragged her relentlessly closer and closer until she was against his chest and both his arms were round her.

"You are entrancing!" he said, "and I have a feeling that while you are undoubtedly a very expert cook, I can teach you a great deal about another art!"

"Let .. me .. go!" Araminta gasped. "Let me .. go .. immediately!"

He laughed and she knew it was a laugh of triumph.

She was aware too that her ineffective struggling excited him.

He was pulling her closer and still closer in an iron-like grip which made her feel helpless and completely impotent against his strength, and now his lips were seeking hers.

Despite the fact that she turned her head from side to side, Araminta knew that it was only a question of time before he conquered her.

She felt his mouth hot and greedy against her cheek.

Because it revolted her with a disgust that she had never known before, she managed to fight him even more violently.

With an almost superhuman effort she thrust him from her and freed herself to run across the room, her breath coming quickly, her heart thumping in her breast.

Lord Rothingham laughed.

"You cannot escape me, my pretty enchantress! I intend to make you mine, and my servants will prevent you from leaving the house."

Araminta stepped behind a high-backed wing-chair to look at him.

Her breath was coming gaspingly from between her lips and she knew as he came towards her that he was both sinister and menacing.

There was a smile on his thick lips and his eyes were narrowing a little.

She knew that what he wanted of her was so degrading, so unspeakable, that she must die rather than submit to it.

She glanced towards the door, feeling he had not spoken idly when he said that he would not let her leave the house.

His servants, whom she already disliked, would definitely refuse to open the front door for her if Lord Rothingham ordered them not to do so.

He was coming nearer and she knew that in another moment he would catch her again and this time there might be no escape.

It was then that she felt a slight draught on her cheek and with a little cry like that of a frightened animal she turned and ran through the french window which opened onto the garden.

She knew as she felt the grass beneath her feet that Lord Rothingham was not far behind, and she thought wildly that as the garden was not large it would be impossible to find anywhere to hide.

What was more, there was a moon creeping up the sky, which, combined with the golden light shining from the windows of the house, made the shadows not dark enough to conceal her.

However she ran blindly away from the house and from the man following her, until, with a throb of horror, she saw the boundary wall ahead.

Then, even as she realised she could go no further, she remembered that the wall on her right bordered with the garden of the Marquis.

She had only a few seconds start and already she could hear Lord Rothingham approaching.

Then she saw propped against the wall there was a big, iron roller with which the gardeners levelled the lawn.

She raced towards it, sprang on the roller and found herself only about two or three feet below the top of the wall.

Araminta had climbed trees, walls and fences in the country ever since she was a child.

It was only a question of seconds before she had heaved herself over the top and dropped down on the other side.

She tore her skirt as she did so, but that was of no consequence.

Even as she dropped she heard Lord Rothingham's voice saying:

"I know where you are hiding, pretty one, and you cannot escape me!"

His determined tone made her feel as if even from the other side of the wall he could reach out and drag her into his arms.

With what should have been a cry for help, but was in fact only a sob because she was so breathless, she started to run across the garden towards the lighted windows of Wayne House, knowing indisputably that there she would be safe.

There were several steps ahead with double french windows opening onto them.

Still terrified, still driven by a panic she could not control, Araminta ran up them and into the room.

She realised that she was in the Library of Wayne House, and as she stood staring wildly about her, her breath coming fitfully between her parted lips, the door opened.

The Marquis came into the room and for a moment stared at her in astonishment.

Then without thinking, without even realising what she was doing, Araminta ran towards him.

"S . save .. me! Please .. save .. me!" she gasped and his arms went round her.

"What has happened? What has upset you?" he asked.

The sound of his voice and the feeling that he was holding her close made it possible for Araminta to stammer in a whisper that he could hardly hear:

"L . Lord Rothingham! H . He is .. trying to .. catch me!"

"Rothingham?" the Marquis exclaimed. "What has he done? What has happened, Araminta?"

"He .. he .. tried to .. kiss me. He said I could not .. escape him. I am .. frightened . . ."

"But you have escaped him," the Marquis said, "and there is no need for you to be frightened any more. I will look after you, Araminta."

She felt an inexpressible relief surge over her. Then as she looked up at him, realising for the first time that she was in his arms, his lips came down on hers!

For a moment she felt only astonishment. Then as his mouth, demanding and insistent, held her captive, she knew now that this was what she had wanted ever since she had first met him.

It was like being lifted into a Heaven which she had not known existed, and the wonder of it was a warm wave flowing through her body, drowning her heart and ending in her lips.

The Marquis's arms tightened and he drew her closer.

Araminta's mouth was very soft beneath his, and she felt as if something magnetic and vibrant drew her heart and soul from her body.

It was a rapture and a joy such as she had never known or believed possible.

'This is love!' she told herself. 'The love I always believed I would find!'

The Marquis released her lips to kiss her eyes, her cheeks, then again her mouth.

Each time he touched her she quivered with a new and miraculous sensation that had something spiritual and divinely perfect about it.

Finally he raised his head and looked down at her.

Araminta's eyes were shining with a radiance such as he had never seen in a woman's eyes before.

"I .. I .. love you!" she whispered a little incoherently.

"I knew what I felt about you last night," the Marquis said, "but I was afraid, my darling, to tell you so."

"I did not .. understand," she murmured.

He held her a little closer.

"If I had suspected that swine would frighten you, I would not have let you go to his house."

"He had .. watched me from his .. window."

"Forget him," the Marquis ordered. "This will never happen again – that I promise you!"

He drew her across the room to a sofa and they sat down side by side, his arm close about her, her head on his shoulder.

"When did you first realise that you loved me?" he asked.

"When you .. kissed me," Araminta whispered and the colour rose in her cheeks.

"And was your first kiss all you hoped it would be?" the Marquis enquired.

"It was wonderful .. more wonderful than I can .. ever tell you," Araminta said.

She hesitated and her grey eyes looked up into his searchingly as she asked:

"It was .. wonderful for you, too?"

"More perfect than any kiss I have ever known," the Marquis answered. "I could not sleep last night for thinking of you. As I expected, you haunted me."

"I felt haunted .. too," Araminta said, "but I did not .. realise it was .. love."

The Marquis smiled.

"You are very wise, my darling, in some ways, but there is a lot I can teach you and it will be the most exciting thing I have ever done!"

"Do you .. mean that?" Araminta asked.

Then his words made her remember Lord Rothingham and she said:

"If your house had not been next door .. if I had not been .. able to .. escape .."

"Forget it," the Marquis said sternly. "Forget everything that happened. It was my fault, Araminta. If I had said last night what I wanted to say, none of this would have happened, and you would not have been cooking for Rothingham."

"There will be no .. need for me to do it any .. more," Araminta replied.

She was thinking of the £50 that she had in her reticule. With what they had already she was certain it would be enough to pay off Harry's debt.

For one moment she wondered if she should tell the Marquis why she was working and why she had wanted to accept the engagement from Lord Rothingham.

Then she knew it would be tantamount to asking him to cancel Harry's debt as he had cancelled Lord Yeoman's, and that would put her in a humiliating position.

Because she loved him she could not take his charity.

Because she loved him, only when the debt was paid would she be able to tell him why she had been forced to earn money.

"What are you thinking about?" the Marquis asked. "And if it is not about me, I forbid it!"

She smiled at him and because she was so happy the whole room seemed to be diffused with a golden light.

"It is .. difficult to think of anything .. but you."

"As I can only think of you," he answered.

His lips moved sensuously over her forehead as if he touched silk.

Then as if the softness of her excited him he was kissing her again, kissing her so that the room seemed to whirl around Araminta and she could not think any more, but only feel and feel . .

The Marquis's lips were on her neck and she felt a little flame of fire run through her veins that was half-pleasure and half-pain.

She moved to turn her face against his shoulder because she was shy that he excited her.

"You are so beautiful," he said. "And your eyes are like pools of mystery in which I can see your heart."

"It is . . yours."

"I want to kiss you from the top of your golden head to the soles of your little feet."

The passion in his voice made Araminta blush.

"I . . must go . . home," she murmured.

She knew as she spoke she had no wish to leave him.

"I cannot bear you to leave me," he said. "You came into my life so unexpectedly! Yet now you fill it to the point when I can think of no-one else."

"You fill . . my life . . too."

"You have bewitched and at the same time inspired me – No woman has ever done that before."

"I am . . glad."

"Oh, my sweet, I want you!"

There was a depth of feeling in the way he spoke which made Araminta say shyly:

"I . . really . . must go."

"I will take you back," he said. "But, darling, tomorrow we will make plans, you and I."

Araminta moved from the shelter of his arms and stood up.

The Marquis rose too, and walked towards the bell-pull which hung beside the mantelpiece, but Araminta cried:

"No! Please . . I cannot let the . . servants see me as I am . . now."

The Marquis looked at her as if he realised for the first time that her struggle with Lord Rothingham had left her in a dishevelled state.

One of her sleeves was half torn from the bodice of her gown, and her skirt was dirty from climbing the wall and also had a jagged tear in it.

Araminta looked down at herself in consternation.

"I have .. left my cloak .. next door."

"You look lovely!" the Marquis said, his eyes on her face. "More lovely than anyone I have ever known before or even imagined could exist!"

He smiled at her tenderly as he went on:

"But we will be very circumspect, my darling. There is a door in the garden wall which leads into the street. We will leave that way and find a hackney carriage in which I can take you home."

"Thank you," Araminta said. "I would not wish .. anyone in this house to know what has occurred."

"They will not do so," the Marquis said confidently. "And I can assure you that Rothingham will not talk because it will make him look a fool. But if he does, I will deal with him!"

His voice was grim.

Then as he moved towards Araminta and took her once again into his arms he said:

"And yet in a way we should be grateful to him because it made you realise I would protect you so that no-one will ever frighten you again."

"I think my Guardian Angel was .. looking after .. me,"

"You look like an angel yourself!" the Marquis replied. "And that is what you will always be — my angel and the keeper of my conscience."

"I told you that you had one," Araminta said with a faint smile.

"I was never sure of it before," the Marquis answered, "but now you have found it for me."

"We belong to .. each other," Araminta whispered. "I feel it would be impossible for us to be closer than we are at this moment."

His lips were on hers and she put her arm around his neck and drew him nearer to her.

The Marquis kissed her masterfully, fiercely and passionately, but she was not afraid. He raised his head.

"I love you!" she whispered.

"I want you to say that not once but a thousand times!" the Marquis replied, "so that I will know it is true."

He put his arm around her shoulders and they moved side by side towards the window. The Marquis picked up a key from his desk.

"Tomorrow," he said, "I will take you to a house I have in Chelsea. It is not really the sort of place in which I would wish to live for long, but to find what I envisage as the right setting for you, my beautiful one, will take time."

He turned his head to kiss her hair before he went on:

"But the house in Chelsea is ready and empty, and you will be safe there for the moment."

Araminta stopped.

"I .. I do not .. understand."

"We want to be together both by day and by night," the Marquis explained. "I cannot imagine it would be easy while you are staying with friends, and it would not be possible for you to come here."

Araminta was very still.

She felt as though an icy hand had taken her heart in its fingers and was slowly squeezing the radiance from it, drop by drop.

"Are you .. asking .." she began, then got no further.

'I am offering you my protection, Araminta," the Marquis said. "I am explaining that when you belong to me no one will insult you, no-one will assault you as Rothingham has done tonight."

His arms tightened as he said:

"You will be mine, and I know that we will be blissfully happy together."

For a moment Araminta felt as if a sudden darkness was rising up from the floor and that she would sink into it and lose consciousness.

Then with an effort she started to walk in the direction

of the window as they had been doing before he spoke.

The Marquis's voice seemed far away as if it came through a fog.

"I will instruct Major Brownlow," he was saying, "to buy or rent a house as near to here as possible. Perhaps in Shepherds Market or in one of the streets around Berkeley Square."

He paused before he continued:

"Then as soon as the season is over we will go abroad. I want to take you to Paris, Araminta, to Rome and perhaps to Greece."

He drew her a little closer as he went on:

"And most certainly we will visit Venice. It is a place for lovers."

Now they were walking across the smooth velvet lawn over which Araminta had run in a panic only a short time before.

Half-way along the garden wall there was a small door which opened onto a quiet street which led off Park Lane.

The Marquis put out the key he had in his hand and unlocked it.

Araminta gave a little exclamation.

"What is it?" he asked.

"I have dropped my handkerchief," she answered. "I can see it over there on the lawn."

She had extracted it from her reticule as they walked along and now in the moonlight it was a touch of white on the smooth green grass.

"I will fetch it for you," the Marquis said.

The door into the street was open and Araminta was standing beside it as he turned back to retrieve her handkerchief.

He did not run but moved quickly with the grace and balance of an athlete.

He picked up the handkerchief and lifted it to his lips.

It smelt of a sweet, fresh fragrance which made him think of spring flowers.

Then as he turned back, holding the small square of soft

linen against his nose, he saw that Araminta must have passed through the open door.

It took the Marquis only a few seconds to follow her, and yet when he reached the street it was empty.

He looked first towards Park Lane, thinking she might have gone that way in search of a carriage.

Puzzled at seeing no sign of her, he turned his head in the other direction, thinking that even in her white gown it might be difficult to see her in the shadowy darkness of the wall.

But in both directions there was only silent emptiness.

The Marquis stood irresolute and was for the first time afraid.

* * * * * *

Araminta had run quicker than she had ever run before to the corner of the garden wall.

By turning left at the end of it she found herself in a mews and still running she turned and twisted going first this way, then that, until she thought she had covered her tracks.

She finally ran into a square where there were several hackney carriages waiting to be engaged, the horses waiting with hay-bags under their noses.

She climbed into the first and, when the cabby asked her somewhat sleepily where she wished to go, she gave him her address.

Only as the horses moved off did she put her hands up to her face and feel that every nerve in her whole body was throbbing with an agony that was indescribable.

Araminta was very innocent, and living in the country she knew little about the excesses and amusements of the social world.

She was of course aware that Kings like Charles II had mistresses. Her history book had taught her what Nell Gwynn's position was in the life of the 'Merrie Monarch'.

She knew too that Madame de Pompadour and Madame de Maintenon were also favourites of the French Kings who already had wives.

But it had never occurred to her that any gentleman she

knew would offer someone he loved a special house and live with her to all intents and purposes as if they were man and wife.

She understood what the Marquis was asking of her, and she did not feel humiliated so much as bewildered and hurt.

She loved him and she had given him her heart from the moment his lips touched hers and she thought in her ignorance that he had felt the same.

Now she told herself that there was really very little difference between what Lord Rothingham had wanted of her and what the Marquis had intended.

'How could I have been so stupid, so naïve,' Araminta asked, 'as to believe that someone in the Marquis's position would be interested, except immorally, in a woman whom he thought of as a servant?'

She thought of all the things she heard spoken of in the past about immorality.

Of the girls who had been condemned in the village for their lustful ways, of the scathing manner in which her mother had referred to some scandal which had been written about in the newspapers.

It had never struck her for one moment that such things concerned her or were ever likely to do, and so she had not been particularly interested.

There had been loose women in the books she had read, but they had been shadowy figures not endowed with flesh and blood.

The men whom they had loved and who had loved them had not in any way resembled the Marquis.

She did not know exactly what a man and a woman did together when they made love. She only knew that real love was part of the Divine and received the blessing of God.

What the Marquis was offering her and what Lord Rothingham had intended was evil and wicked, the temptation of Satan.

Araminta shut her eyes.

She was not crying. She felt as if her whole being had dried up until she was a desert of dead sand.

'I love .. him!' she told herself. 'But what he feels for .. me is not .. love.'

London was no longer a place of entertainment and amusement, an El Dorado to which she had journeyed so joyously when they had left Bedfordshire.

It had become horrible, menacing, unclean – as she knew now the private room to which the Marquis had taken her the previous evening was unclean.

She felt as if everything that had happened had not hurt her physically as it might have done. But that mentally she had been crucified.

It was like her gown which had once been spotlessly white and was now besmeared with dirt and torn, so that she was ashamed, as she stepped out of the carriage to pay the cabby, in case he should notice her appearance.

She ran up the steps to let herself in through the door.

She felt as she shut it behind her that she was shutting out something that was encroaching upon her, something that, if she was not careful, would destroy her.

She stood for a moment in the hall which was lit only by one candle standing on a table at the bottom of the staircase.

She looked at it and saw beside it was a hat which she recognised as Harry's.

She ran to the sitting-room, flung open the door and there, sitting talking together, were her brother and Caro.

They looked up as Araminta entered, then as they saw her appearance they both rose to their feet.

"Araminta! What has happened?" Caro cried.

But Araminta's eyes were on Harry's face, and pulling at the ribbons which had tied her reticule to her left wrist she released them and ran towards him.

"There is .. £50 here! £50. Harry! With all we have already .. it should be enough. I cannot .. do any more. It is .. impossible .. quite .. quite impossible! We must .. go .. home!"

CHAPTER SEVEN

The General, having finished breakfast, had settled down with *The Morning Post* when Hawkins came into the room.

"The Marquis of Wayne to see you, Sir!"

"Again?" the General exclaimed.

He glanced at the clock with a surprised expression in his eyes.

He was not used to such early callers, but he said reluctantly:

"Very well, Hawkins. Show His Lordship in."

A few seconds later the Marquis appeared, as usual exquisitely dressed, but the General thought that he looked thinner and there was something drawn about his face that he had not noticed previously.

"Do not get up, General," the Marquis said as the General was about to rise. "I apologise for calling at such an hour."

The General did not reply, he merely sat back in his chair with his shrewd eyes on the Marquis's face.

There was no doubt that he did in fact look different from when he had called ten days earlier.

"I have come to you in desperation!" the Marquis said after a moment.

He did not sit, but stood facing the older man, and there was an expression on his face which the General did not understand.

"I told you, Wayne, on the last occasion on which you visited me," the General replied crisply, "that I have no intention of disclosing to you the whereabouts of Araminta – Bouvais. Had she wished you to know where she was, she would undoubtedly have communicated with you."

The Marquis crossed the room restlessly as if he was debating something with himself. Then he said:

"I was not entirely honest with you, General, the last time we talked I think you had the impression that I wished to find Miss Bouvais because she had not kept her engagement with me as – a cook."

The General said nothing and after a moment the Marquis continued:

"I am not interested in her cooking, but in – her!"

He spoke as if it was an effort to say the words. Then as he waited the General answered:

"Whatever your reasons, the situation, as far as I am concerned, remains unaltered.'

"But I must find her!"

The Marquis spoke violently, his voice raised. Then with an effort at self-control he said:

"I know you do not like me, General. You have always been fair and just, but I was well aware that there was no warmth in our relationship."

"You were a good soldier," the General remarked.

"And now that I am no longer under your command, you feel there is no reason for us to be anything more than members of the same Club?"

The General did not reply, and after a moment the Marquis said:

"But I desperately need help, and you are in fact the only person who can help me."

There was an appeal in the Marquis's words which the General, who had listened to the pleadings of many different people, did not miss.

"I am sorry, Wayne," he said with a kinder note in his voice, "but I have given my word of honour, and you would not expect me to break it."

"Since I last saw you," the Marquis continued as if he had not spoken, "I have journeyed to Yorkshire."

He saw the question in the General's eyes and explained:

"To visit Yeoman. I do not know if Araminta told you, but she persuaded me to cancel a debt he owed me."

The Marquis gave a short laugh that had no humour in it.

"No-one but Araminta could have made me do such a thing and do it willingly! But Yeoman has been sworn to

145

silence just as you have, and he will not tell me where she is."

The Marquis drew a deep breath before he added:

"The house where I left her the night she had supper with me is empty. No-one has lived in it for three years."

He threw out his hands in a gesture of helplessness.

"Where else can I go? Where else can I seek for her unless you help me?"

He knew by the General's attitude that he would not alter his decision.

The Marquis walked across the room and back again.

"I want to tell you something," he said in a low tone, "something I have never told anyone else."

"I am listening," the General said quietly.

"When I was seventeen," the Marquis began, "my father wished to send me on the Grand Tour, but as we were at war with Napoleon it was obviously impossible. He therefore engaged a tutor recommended to act as my companion during the school holiday."

He paused before he continued:

"Roland Hindley was the most interesting and attractive man I had ever met. He was twenty-four and was reading for the Bar, but as his parents were poor he was compelled to earn money by coaching pupils while he continued with his own studies."

The Marquis again walked backwards and forwards across the room as he talked.

"Roland was a first class athlete. He could fence, he was an excellent shot, he was a pugilist! He also rode in a manner which made me ashamed that I was not a better horseman."

The Marquis glanced at the General as if to be sure he was listening and went on:

"We could not go to Europe, but we travelled all over the British Isles. We rode and hunted in Ireland, we stalked in Scotland, we climbed Snowdon. Everything I did with Roland was a delight.

"He took the place of the brother which as an only child I never had; he also stimulated my brain and led me to enjoy subjects which previously I had thought a bore.

146

"He stayed with us until my last year at Eton, when he came to Wayne for Christmas."

The Marquis was silent for a few seconds before he continued:

"You may not be aware that my father was very much older than my mother. She married him when she was only seventeen, and I was born the following year.

"She was so gay and beautiful that I never thought of her as being very much older than I was."

The Marquis's voice sharpened as he said:

"I suppose, being young, I was very obtuse. That Christmas my father was ill and confined to his room, but the house seemed to be filled with happiness."

He appeared to be looking back into the past as he went on:

"My mother joined Roland and me when we skated on the lake, tobogganed down the snow-covered slopes of the park, and rode through the woods. In the evening we would group round the piano and sing old songs and ballads to my mother's accompaniment."

There was a raw note in the Marquis's voice as he said:

"I never had the slightest suspicion of what was happening until I found a note which had been slipped under my door very early one morning."

"They had run away together!" the General exclaimed.

"They had left for Roland's home in Cornwall. My mother asked me to inform my father that she would not come back."

"Surely that was rather cruel?" the General remarked.

"I was determined to stop her," the Marquis said. "I dressed, and hurried to the stables where I learnt that she and Roland had left at dawn."

The Marquis turned his back on the General to stare with sightless eyes out of the window.

"I was an hour behind them, but I rode across country."

"What happened?"

"There had been a sharp frost the night before and the roads were icy. The curricule in which my mother and

147

Roland were driving collided with a stage-coach on a bend about fifteen miles from home!"

"They were injured!"

"They were both dead!"

There was a long silence. Then the General asked:

"What did you do?"

"I went home, told my father that the three of us had planned a visit to a neighbouring town. My mother and Roland were driving, I was to ride over the fields and could therefore start later."

"He had no suspicion of anything else?"

"No-one had," the Marquis replied. "No-one ever suspected that my story was not factual."

The General waited.

"I have told you this," the Marquis said after a moment, "so that you will understand why I swore to myself that never again would I be hurt in such a way."

"You felt you had been betrayed?" the General asked perceptively.

"Of course I felt that," the Marquis answered harshly. "My mother was prepared to abandon me, the man I had loved as a brother and worshipped as a hero with the idealism of youth was ready to break up my home and destroy my father's happiness! What do you think I felt?"

The General did not answer and after a moment the Marquis said more quietly:

"Now perhaps you understand why people speak of my being aloof, or as Araminta described it, as standing apart from life."

He turned again towards the window.

"The shock of what happened all those years ago had a profound effect upon me. Because of it I have never, General – and this is the truth – made advances to or accepted favours from a married woman. In fact, where women are concerned I have confined myself to Cyprians who know the rules of the game."

The General's eyes rested on the back of the Marquis's head.

He could understand now why many beautiful ladies of

the *Beau Monde* were often bitter about the Marquis.

There was nothing more frustrating to a woman than to have her overtures refused.

There was a pause before the Marquis said:

"I have never told a woman I loved her, because I have never loved one until – now."

Again there was silence.

"I have wanted love – God knows I have hungered for it – but I would not admit it to myself."

The General would have spoken, but the Marquis went on in a low voice:

"That was why I did not understand what Araminta meant to me, not until I had lost her."

"What does she mean to you?" the General asked.

The Marquis turned and walked to stand in front of him, as if he were a soldier under his command.

"I wish to marry her! Now will you tell me where I can find her?"

"You mean that, knowing nothing about her family?"

"It does not matter a damn what Araminta's family is like," the Marquis replied, "it is what she is that matters to me."

The General looked at him with compassion in his eyes.

He had dealt with men all his life and knew when they were sincere. He knew too when a man spoke from the heart without reserve.

"I have given my word and you will appreciate that it cannot be broken," he said slowly after a moment. "But I would suggest that young Sinclair might be able to help you."

"Sinclair?" the Marquis questioned. "Sinclair? Do you mean Harry Sinclair who owed me some money! Brownlow told me he has paid off his debt."

"Yes, Harry Sinclair. White's will doubtless have his address."

The Marquis gave a deep sigh which seemed to come from the very depths of his being.

"Thank you, General. If I find Araminta, you will never regret having helped me."

He went from the room as if he was suddenly in a great hurry and the General stared after him reflectively.

Then his old eyes twinkled and there was a smile on his lips.

He had never before found the Marquis of Wayne so likeable.

. . . . . .

"There! Papa's book is finished!" Caro cried on a note of triumph.

"I wonder if there will be a sale for it," Araminta pondered.

"I do not see why not," Caro said almost defiantly. "After all, Mrs. Glass's are out of date and, as you found yourself, Araminta, people are far more interested in good cooking than they were a few years ago."

"Well, we can but try," Araminta said without much hope in her voice. "Harry can take it to the publishers."

"Harry cannot afford to go to London at the moment," Caro retorted. "We had much better post it."

"Yes, of course," Araminta agreed.

The door opened and Caro gave a little cry.

"Speak of the devil!"

Harry came into the room.

"If you are talking about me, there is nothing to say. One day is just like another in this benighted hole!"

"Do not let Mama hear you," Araminta begged. "You know it upsets her if you are not happy. And anyway she has a headache."

"Why can I not find something to do?" Harry asked angrily, then added in a different tone: "I am going to swallow my pride and ask Farmer Upton if he will let me break in some horses which he bought last week at the Fair."

"I am sure he would be delighted," Caro replied. "He is far too busy and too heavy-handed to do much with them himself."

"That is what I thought," Harry remarked. "If I do not find something to fill my days I shall go mad!"

"Go and talk to Farmer Upton," Araminta interposed.

"He has always had a soft spot for you, Harry, ever since you were a little boy."

"He has told me I can shoot over his land whenever I wish to."

Caro gave a shout.

"Then for goodness sake, go and shoot something for the pot!"

"It is really the wrong time of year."

"Never mind about that! A rabbit would be very welcome do you not agree, Araminta?"

Araminta did not reply.

She was remembering how the Marquis had laughed when she had discovered that '*Poulet Suprême Louis*' had been made with rabbit and not chicken.

Then she told herself that there was no use thinking of what had happened in the past. It was over and done with and she must concern herself with the future.

"A rabbit would be delicious. Or even rook-pie might be a change."

"I see you are both determined to keep me busy," Harry said with a smile. "I will go and see Farmer Upton this afternoon and take my gun with me."

"And just be careful what you're a-doing with it!" a voice said from the door.

"I am a very safe shot, Hannah," Harry retorted as the old maid came into the room.

"So I should hope!" Hannah sniffed. "I never did like fire-arms, nasty, dangerous things!"

She was carrying a glass of milk in her hand and she set it down in front of Araminta.

"Oh, no, Hannah!" Araminta exclaimed. "I cannot drink any more milk, I cannot really!"

"You'll drink it and like it, Miss Araminta," Hannah said sharply. "I've already taken two inches out of your gowns, and your face is all eyes! If you don't believe me look in the mirror!"

"It is true," Caro agreed. "You have grown much too thin, Araminta, and you do not eat enough to keep a mouse alive!"

"Please stop bullying me," Araminta pleaded.

She picked up the glass of milk and drank it obediently.

Hannah took the empty glass and opened the door.

"I'm making your favourite, shepherd's pie, for luncheon, Miss Araminta, so kindly do justice to it."

She moved half way into the Hall as she was speaking, then gave an exclamation which they all heard.

"Who can this be arriving?" she questioned. "Are you expecting anyone, Master Harry?"

Harry followed Hannah from the room.

"Good God!" his sisters heard him ejaculate and Caro ran to join him.

"Look at those horses," she cried, "and that Phaeton! Who is it, Harry?"

"I think – I am sure," Harry replied, "that it is the Marquis of Wayne!"

Araminta who had remained seated at the table sprang to her feet.

She joined her brother and sister in the Hall, then cried in a frantic tone:

"He must not know that I am here! You must not tell him who I am! Promise me, Harry .. promise that you will swear that you have no .. knowledge of .. Miss Bouvais?"

Her brother did not answer and after a second Araminta said:

"I will go and hide in the garden so that there is no chance of his catching a .. glimpse of me. Thank goodness he cannot see Mama. Promise Harry .. and .. be careful .. be very careful what you say!"

As she spoke the last words she was running towards the garden door which opened at the back of the house and was not in sight of the drive.

Araminta let herself out, then ran through the shrubs which bordered the badly cut lawn and led down to the stream at the end of the garden.

Here there was an arbour where the children had always hidden when they were small. A wooden seat was surrounded by flowering shrubs and fragrant with the scent of honeysuckle and climbing roses.

There were some rough steps leading down to the water's edge where they had caught 'tiddlers' when they were children and sailed paper boats.

Araminta was breathless when she reached the arbour but it was not only because she had been running that her heart was beating so tumultuously.

Why had the Marquis come to their home, she wondered, and how did he know where it was?

She thought that his business must in fact be with Harry.

But why, when the £600 had been handed over to Major Brownlow nearly two weeks ago?

Could Harry have got into more trouble?

Suppose he owed more than they had paid?

There was still a little left from the sale of Lady Sinclair's precious engagement ring, but it was really only enough to keep as a nest-egg against illness or for Harry when he became too restless to tolerate the country any longer.

'We cannot find any more!' Araminta thought despairingly.

She sat down on the wooden seat and wondered what the Marquis would have thought if she had been waiting for him when Hannah showed him into the drawing-room.

As presumably he had come to see Harry, he would be surprised and perhaps embarrassed to find her there.

He would never know, Araminta thought, what she had suffered these past weeks since she had run away from him.

Every night she cried herself to sleep.

Every night in the darkness of her bed-room she could see his handsome face, his grey eyes looking into hers, and feel his lips take possession of her.

Sometimes she felt that the pain of being apart from him was so intense, so agonising, that she would go back to London and accept any terms he offered just as long as she could be with him.

Then she told herself that even her love would not survive in such circumstances.

Love that was perfect would not flourish on an evil foundation.

If she was suffering now, she would suffer even more

intensely when the moment came for the Marquis to discard her because she no longer interested him.

But it was difficult to be sensible and logical when her whole body ached for him, when there were tears running down her cheeks and she could only murmur despairingly:

"I love .. you! I love .. you!"

Sitting on the wooden seat, staring at the sun glinting on the stream below, Araminta felt that the future held no sunshine, no hope.

Ahead were only long years of drab, grey poverty, loneliness and that insistent, aching pain of loss.

She found it difficult to stay in hiding.

She wanted to run back to the house, to peep through the windows, to have one glimpse of the Marquis, just one, before she steeled herself to the knowledge that she would never see him again.

She heard footsteps approaching, realised they were a man's and thought it must be Harry coming to tell her that the Marquis had left.

To hide the tears in her eyes she rose to her feet to walk to the water's edge.

She heard someone come through the bushes.

"He has .. gone?" she asked in a low voice.

There was no answer.

She turned round to find that it was not Harry standing facing her but the Marquis!

He seemed to her to be taller, larger and even better-looking than she remembered, and as their eyes met she knew it was impossible to move and equally impossible to breathe.

"Araminta!"

His voice was low and deep and yet there was an irrepressible lilt in it.

"I have found you! I have found you, when I had almost given up hope!"

"Why .. are you .. here?"

It was so difficult to speak that she thought he could not have heard what she said. But he had heard, though misunderstood her question.

"Harry told me where you were hiding."

"I told him .. not to tell .. you."

The Marquis smiled faintly.

"He tried to deny all knowledge of you, but it was impossible for him to do so, once I had been shown into the drawing-room."

Araminta looked puzzled.

"There is a portrait of you over the mantelpiece."

"That .. is a picture of .. Mama."

"You are very like her."

Araminta felt as if they were talking in a dream, conversing with their lips while their hearts said something quite different.

"Why did you .. come to see .. Harry?" she asked at length.

"I believed he might help me to find you. I had to ask you, Araminta, to forgive me."

Because she could not look into his eyes any longer Araminta turned aside to stare down at the gold-flecked stream.

She felt him come nearer to her.

"Please forgive me, my darling," the Marquis said in a low voice. "Forgive me, and let me tell you how desperately ashamed I am."

Araminta did not move and after a moment he said:

"I have no excuse – no real excuse – for behaving like a cad, except that I have never met anyone like you before, and have never, and this is the truth, Araminta, been in love until now."

Araminta drew in her breath.

Then she was still as if she dared not move in case she broke the spell that enveloped her.

There was a note in the Marquis's voice which she had never heard before.

It had a depth of feeling which made her vibrate as if to some strange and magical music.

"I love you, my precious little Araminta, and it will take me a whole life-time to tell you how much! Are you prepared to spend your life with me?"

Still Araminta could not move and the Marquis said insistently:

"I am asking you to marry me, my darling!"

Araminta turned her head to look at him, her eyes wide and troubled, her lips trembling a little.

"Why are you .. asking .. me?"

"Because I cannot live without you," the Marquis answered. "Because I was such a fool that I did not understand what you meant to me until you vanished."

He moved a little nearer still, but did not touch her.

"Can you forget what I said to you? Can we go back to that moment when I kissed you. It was the first time for you and the first time I had known a kiss could be so wonderful – so perfect."

Araminta's eyes looked into his, then she said in a voice he could hardly hear:

"Are you .. are you .. certain that you .. want me?"

The Marquis made a little sound that was half a laugh and half a groan, then he put his arms gently around her and pulled her close to him.

"You do not know the tortures I have been through thinking about you and wondering if I would ever find you again, thinking that perhaps you hated me."

Araminta did not speak and he asked very softly:

"Did you miss me just a little, my lovely one?"

"I .. wanted to .. die!" Araminta whispered.

"My sweet! My darling! I will make it up to you, but I can never forgive myself for having made you unhappy."

Very slowly the Marquis bent his head and his lips found Araminta's.

He kissed her, as a man might kiss a flower, then with Araminta's lips soft beneath his as he felt a little quiver go through her, his kiss became more demanding, more insistent.

"I love you! I love you, Araminta, with all my heart and with all my soul."

He kissed her again.

Now she felt as if he gave her himself, and the wonder of

being in his arms was more intense and more ecstatic than she had ever imagined it could be.

There was something spiritual and holy in their closeness, something which she knew in her heart was divine.

There were tears of sheer happiness in Araminta's eyes and the Marquis kissed them away.

Then he kissed her cheeks and again her lips and all the time there was something that was different in his touch.

It was so wonderful that Araminta clung to him as if he might vanish.

He drew her closer and closer, and then he said, echoing the words in her own mind:

"I cannot be without you any longer, Araminta! How soon will you marry me? How soon can we be together?"

"I .. want to be .. with you."

"That, my darling, is the right answer, and I feel already as if I have waited an eternity for you."

"I .. thought I would .. never see you .. again."

"I would have gone on searching for you," the Marquis said. "As long as you were alive I was sure that sooner or later I would find you; and if you were dead I would have known it."

He gave a little laugh.

"You haunted me enough as it was! I would lie awake every night going over every word we said to each other, seeing your face, looking into your eyes and feeling your lips beneath mine."

"That .. is what .."

Araminta stopped.

"What were you going to say?" he asked.

The colour rose in her cheeks and she hid her face in his shoulder.

"That is .. what I also .. felt at .. night," she whispered, "that you .. were with me, that you .. were .. kissing me."

The Marquis held her so tightly that it was painful.

"Our minds were close, but that is not enough, my sweet, I want you in my arms, I want you to belong to me. I want to be certain you are mine."

"That is .. what I want .. too."

157

"Tell me you love me! I want to be sure of it."

"I .. love .. you."

"And you forgive me?"

"You know .. I do."

"I meant to go down on my knees to show you how desperately sorry I am."

"I would .. rather .. you held me .. like this."

"I want you closer. I want to possess every precious piece of you, for ever."

"I am .. yours .. you know I .. belong to you."

"Darling, my perfect, incredibly beautiful little love!"

The Marquis kissed her until Araminta could not breathe. Then he looked down into her shining eyes.

He had never believed a woman could look so brilliantly happy, with an unearthly radiance which transformed her.

"I love you!" he said, and it was a vow rather than a statement. He put his cheek against hers as he said:

"Shall we go and talk to Harry? If he is back!"

"If he is back!" Araminta questioned in surprise. "Where has he gone?"

"He is driving my Phaeton," the Marquis replied. "I have already told him that he can ride or drive every horse in my stable, as long as he will give his blessing to our marriage."

He looked down at her and said:

"Harry has told me how wonderful and brave you were in raising the money to pay me. Could fate have concocted a more bizarre way for us to meet? That you should work for me to pay me back with my own money the debt Harry owed me?"

"I thought of .. telling you," Araminta said, "but I knew that you would then try to .. cancel the debt .. and because it was one of .. honour it had to be .. paid."

"I am not going to regret that I won that money from Harry," the Marquis said, "for the simple reason that if I had not done so I would never have met you, my precious love. But I promise that when we are married I shall have no wish to waste my time at the gaming tables when I might be with you."

He saw the question in Araminta's eyes and added:

"And of course, fighting the causes you wish me to champion in the House of Lords."

"You will do .. that?"

"I have already composed my speech on the state of agriculture," he answered. "I had plenty of time to think of one when I was journeying to Yorkshire."

"To Yorkshire?"

"I can assure you that Lord Yeoman kept his promise," the Marquis smiled. "He would not reveal where he left you the night he took you home."

Araminta gave a little sigh.

"I seem to have put you to a great deal of .. trouble."

"You caused me more misery and unhappiness than I have ever known in my whole life!" the Marquis said. "But since there was no-one to blame but myself I have become very humble, Araminta."

"I do not want you changed!" Araminta cried, "I love you as you are. I feel as if I have loved you all my life, and you have always been near me."

She gave him a smile of sheer happiness and went on:

"We have known each other for such a short time, and yet time has really nothing to do with it."

"We are a part of each other," the Marquis said quietly. "So much a part, my precious darling, that when you left me I was only half a man. Now you have made me whole again."

He sought her lips with a demanding passion.

She felt a thrill run through her because he was so masterful.

Then he took his arms from her and said:

"Let me look at you! Let me be certain that you are everything I remember and a thousand times more beautiful!"

"You are .. embarrassing .. me," Araminta blushed.

"You are so lovely, so perfect," the Marquis said. "It is difficult to imagine anything could improve you! But, my darling, you shall have the gowns you gave up for Harry – the most beautiful gowns that not only London can provide, but also Paris."

He pulled Araminta into his arms again as he said:

"We are going to Paris, my precious, on our honeymoon. Just as we will go to Rome and to Venice. I not only want you alone, but I shall also be so proud to introduce my friends to my wife."

"Perhaps," Araminta said in a low voice, "they will think you should have .. married someone more .. important .. someone in the social world to which you .. belong."

"My true friends will be glad that I have found the woman I love, and who loves me," the Marquis said solemnly. "What the rest thinks is of no consequence."

"I do .. love you!" Araminta murmured.

"And I adore and worship you," he answered. "I have never felt like this before, Araminta. I have never known what it is to feel very humble and yet overwhelmingly proud and triumphant because I have found what most men fail to find."

His lips were very near to Araminta's as he said:

"It is my sweet, something for which all men hunger, all men long for and for which all men search. It is love – the real love which unites two people so that they become one."

"And that .. is what has .. happened to us!"

"That is what will happen completely and irrevocably when we are married," the Marquis promised. "And because we have found love we are truly blessed, my Sweetheart, and we shall, I swear, be eternally happy."

His mouth was on hers at the last word.

"I shall never again be hungry for love," he murmured.

Then he lifted her above the world into the golden sunlight.

It was so radiant, so ecstatic and so rapturous that there were no words for the wonder and perfection of a pure and undefiled love.